D0422316

THE
TWO POUND
TRAM

THE
TWO POUND
TRAM

William Newton

BLOOMSBURY

First published 2003

Copyright © 2003 by William Newton

The moral right of the author has been asserted

Bloomsbury Publishing Plc, 38 Soho Square,
London WID 3HB

A CIP catalogue record for this book
is available from the British Library

ISBN 0 7475 6697 6

Typeset by Hewer Text Ltd, Edinburgh
Printed in Great Britain by Clays Ltd, St Ives plc

Chapter One

THIS IS THE STORY of my brother Duncan. I write it because I am able to do so and he for various reasons is not. I am Wilfred, a year and a half the younger. We were born in the 1920s and grew up in the '30s. After that our lives suddenly changed, displaced by new events as the war unfolded and finally ended. It is therefore a story which starts in a world now vanished.

We lived in Sussex not far from the sea in a house called Greenacres, a name which was apt, for its spacious grounds were where most of our life's events took place; you could say that it was also the basis of our independence. Of our father and mother we saw little except at lunch-time on Wednesdays, which was allotted entirely to ourselves and to all practical matters arising from us. These had to be settled then and there. The rest of their life we were not part of; it took place somewhere else, on golf courses and at weekend parties which we knew about only from fragments of their conversation which we happened to overhear. Our world was the domestic one, where our fellow inhabitants, who provided our care, our conversation and quite a lot of our education, were the two housemaids and the cook.

The arrangements of the Scrutton family were by no means unusual for the time, and even if we had thought about them, which we didn't, I doubt if we would have complained. Nor does this mean that we did not admire our parents, far from it, because we certainly did admire them, especially our mother. Of our mother the most vivid recollection would certainly be of her in her car, an enormous machine with an open top called a Hispano-Suiza. In it she swept about our neighbourhood, day or night, at breakneck speed, instantly recognisable in one of her cloche hats.

The Hispano-Suiza was cause for the greatest excitement of our childhood, because sometimes Mother had the impulse to include us in her expeditions, and then behind her on the back seat, and clutching the straps behind the door pillars thoughtfully provided by the car's maker for nervous passengers, we sailed into the unknown; down the Sussex lanes we went, heavy with the smell of tamarisk, and afterwards, as she warmed to the expedition, onwards into the Downs themselves. In this fashion we spanned the breadth of Sussex, from Chancton-bury and Alfriston on one side to Cowdray Ruin and Swanbourne Lake on the other, all spread out before us like a magical map. For me it was especially dear because I always sat behind Mother as she drove, which was about the nearest I ever got to her, and I could inhale her perfume which made me quite stupefied.

However, such close contact was fleeting, and what attention she gave us was usually directed towards Duncan, but the curious fact is that Duncan always made a display of boredom and withdrew from such encounters. This made him seem superhuman to my childish percep-tion. Privately I revelled in the fact that I had been christened Wilfred in honour of mother's two brothers, William and Frederick, both of whom were killed in the Great War. For some reason our father never called me Wilfred; instead when he did address me I was always 'Number Two'. I thought that this must be a naval expression and I spent much time trying to be officer-like in my conduct and manner. However, this passed without his notice.

In general it was not Father's habit to show affection to either of us, but he did take a close interest in our education, and here I was greatly relieved that it was Duncan and not myself who was the subject of his attention. This happened on the occasions when Father and Mother spent the weekend at Greenacres, and on Sundays, after lunch had been cleared away, Duncan would be sent for to go to the hall. To this day I can never understand why it was called the hall when plainly it was the dining room and was where all their friends gathered when they were at home. It was a large and somewhat frightening room, dark on account of all the panelling and old pictures, and Mother and Father sat at either end of a a very long table.

As Duncan entered Mother would rise and sit at a smaller table where her cards were laid out for patience, Duncan taking her place at the end. Then the questions started, first sums and after that Latin. The memory of Duncan facing these onslaughts for half an hour or more scares me to this day, but he was clever and had all the answers. Afterwards he would emerge still aglow, as though he had scored a goal at football, and would relate it question by question and repeat all the answers he had given. Even Father appeared elated and seemed to forgive Duncan for his left-handedness – except when he held his knife and fork the wrong way round, for that Father could not abide.

At times when Duncan was enduring these cross-examinations I drifted into the scullery to talk to Edith, who did the washing-up, or best of all to the kitchen, where Mrs Marrow, our cook, would tell me stories of the wonderful houses where she had worked. It seemed unfair that I should be thus engrossed while Duncan had to answer his questions in the hall, but curiously he did not see it that way. To him it was a challenge he loved to rise to, and from that time he was to me a hero whom no other human being could match.

In one of the farther reaches of Greenacres there stood an old railway carriage, set there perhaps by some previous occupant and used as a potting shed. It was for us an enduring magnet, a mystery, a miracle, and it gradually became in our emerging consciousness a sort of home to be. The first compartment we colonised became our workshop, where we made carts from bits of discarded bicycles and other items mechanical and electrical, with both of which sorts Duncan possessed an extraordinary ingenuity. Our second compartment came later; it also bore on its windows the letters LB & SCR, frosted on the glass, proclaiming the company that had built it and run it once as part of a train the London, Brighton and South Coast Railway. Its one remaining seat had a cushion made of dark and buttoned leather, and here we cooked our meals – pigeons, rooks or other birds as came to hand, and especially rabbits, all being the victims of our catapults.

We carried catapults with us on all occasions, and Duncan in particular had a remarkable eye for a moving target. He was a dead shot at anything less than thirty yards away and occasionally hit at twice that distance. In our woods or when we took our bicycles and went on expeditions it was therefore Duncan who did most of the hunting and I who did the cooking.

We attended, though not quite every day, a school in Worthing run by a Mr Potts, also known to the boys as Stinker Potts. After hours, if it was summer, we would cycle to the Downs to catch butterflies for our collection which was substantial, and all carefully mounted on pins and placed in butterfly boxes lined with cork. We had much knowledge of this subject, most of it derived from *Butterflies of the British Isles* by R. South. We had no great need of money, but in the winter months we cut down trees which were out of sight at the edges of our grounds, also sometimes just beyond the edges. These we sawed into logs with a cross-cut saw and loaded on to one of our carts to sell to the neighbour-hood.

But our dream, our obsession, was to own a tram.

It all started with an advertisement on the front page of the *Daily Mail* which showed a picture of a London tram with the words: 'Trams surplus to the requirements of the London Omnibus and Tramcar Company for sale at their depot at Acton, London W6, for £2 each.'

I doubt if there was a day afterwards when the tram did not enter our conversation.

An unfortunate event now happened which changed the course of both our lives. Duncan began to have terrible headaches and he rapidly became seriously ill and then unconscious. A doctor came and pronounced it to be brain fever and directed that he must be nursed in a darkened room. Day and night nurses came and poultices of something called antiphlogistin were applied to Duncan's neck, so that the smell of them spread all through the house and lingered there. Our mother slept in his room. In the opinion of the doctor Duncan had only a short time to live and even if he did survive he would be blind or deaf or both. It was a desolate time and for me very hard to bear, for I was banished to the furthermost part of the house for fear that I, too, would contract the illness.

For two weeks Duncan was unconscious and the issue remained in doubt, but then he began to recover. Visitors were allowed and I was readmitted to the sick room, but I was appalled, for it was no longer the Duncan I had known; he had aged by at least ten years and his hair was grey. At least he had not lost his sight nor even his hearing, as his manner and movements showed. What he had lost was the power of speech. He was completely dumb.

Chapter Two

SPECIALISTS WERE SUMMONED and finally Lord Dawson, the most famous doctor in the land, came from London; but not even he could alter Duncan's state. A speech therapist was sent for and started to teach Duncan and our mother the sign language used by deaf and dumb people. They tried valiantly, and I myself took part in the lessons, but this was not attended by success and after a while first our mother and then the therapist gave up the attempt.

We were left on our own. It was then that I became aware that, although Duncan could not speak, he was quite normal in every other respect; in fact, he was as bright as a button. We started making faces at each other. Little by little he learnt to show what he wanted by glances and gestures which I copied and then put into words. These gestures speedily became more elaborate, so that in making them he used almost every part of his body. From that time on his recovery was rapid, and by the time his strength had returned we had developed a language of our own. The only trouble was that it was a private language which only we understood.

At this point Duncan's speech, or a fragment of it, did indeed begin to return and this was another trouble for it consisted only of the word 'wasit' – this was what it generally sounded like, although it varied. It also seemed to come out without Duncan's intending it, and generally without there being any sense in his saying it. It took me rather longer to realise that he only said it after I had said something which had the word 'was' in it and so it seemed to be a sort of automatic response. At first it seemed to irritate Duncan that he couldn't stop himself, and he would try to do so by putting his hand over his mouth. When this didn't work he tried other means, varying the way he said it or even putting it into my conversation as if it made sense, which it didn't. He managed to change it slightly so that at times it came out as 'washit' or 'watchit'.

Unfortunately, this was all the speech that he recovered.

Gradually our life returned to what it had been before Duncan's illness. We were able to resume our old habits, and among other things it was clear that Duncan's accuracy with his catapult was unchanged. We celebrated with a fine boiled chicken.

Duncan was even returned to school, although this was not a great success. He proved able to write down words and to do his sums as the masters directed, but his inability to answer questions seemed to them somehow unsatisfactory. At first it was thought that he was exceptionally quiet on account of having been so ill, and his grave and mature bearing seemed to support this, but by degrees it began to be realised that something was amiss. Only Mr Potts persisted in shouting at Duncan in the belief that this would wake him up.

It scarcely helped that Duncan, in letting out his 'wasits', appeared to be questioning, or even contrary. Several of the younger masters grasped after a while that it was best to keep the word 'was' out of their sentences. The boys, on the other hand, spotted it at once and during the mid-morning breaks would form a line behind him and circle the school yard repeating 'was, was, was' in chorus. In due course Duncan would oblige with 'wasit' and then they changed to 'wash, wash, wash' or other ingenious variations. It became the game to play.

He became 'Wasit' Scrutton, and two lines were formed and began to go round the courtyard, one chanting, 'Was it Scrutton?' and the other replying, 'Yes, it was.' It was just like a football crowd. They never tired of it, and what with his grave manner and grown-up appearance Duncan was soon the most popular boy in the school.

It did not pass unnoticed and Mr Potts, in particular, became visibly irritated. He summoned Duncan to his study and told him in no uncertain terms that he must stop this silly nonsense. He added that if he did not do so, and promptly, then he, Mr Potts, would have to resort to certain measures. He quite failed to realise that the trick was not to say 'was' to Duncan in the first place.

Matters came to a head during a history lesson. History was Mr Potts's special subject and therefore history lessons took place in the main hall, where the entire school was assembled. Those who could sat at desks, the remainder on chairs placed at the sides, and beyond these stood any of the junior masters who were not otherwise occupied.

The class fell to silence as Mr Potts entered and climbed the step of the platform, on which a desk had been placed for him. He began his lecture.

'Our subject is the war between the King and Oliver Cromwell. At heart King Charles the First was a good man.'

'Was shit,' said Duncan promptly.

Mr Potts was taken aback, and for a moment there was a silence broken only by the noise of his pince-nez which fell off his nose and on to the floor with a clatter.

A titter ran round the hall and several of the masters standing at the side were seen to grin, although they very quickly hid their grins behind their hands. One boy had the temerity to bang the lid of his desk as a sign of approval, and the others followed. Mr Potts realised that he had a rebellion on his hands. He responded in the only way he knew: he resolved to hit his way out of trouble. He seized from the front of his desk the cane that lay there mainly for ceremonial, and advanced down the hall. He seized Duncan by the ear, led him back to the desk, bent him over it and, still holding his ear, administered some colossal thwacks.

The class was at first subdued but then it grew bolder and boys started banging the tops of the desks in unison as the blows fell.

It was too much for Mr Potts. He picked up his glasses from the floor where they had fallen and strode out, passing as he did so the line of junior masters, where he paused and spat out, 'Grimes, take over the class.' The unfortunate Mr Grimes had been just too slow in concealing his grin.

A state of war now existed between Mr Potts and Duncan, and nothing could avert the battles that were to follow. It was a war which Mr Potts was determined to win, and he was nothing if not consistent. His plan and its execution all took place in his study.

This room had walls which were panelled up to the ceiling, and upon the polished wood like trophies there hung a collection of instruments of correction inherited and added to by a succession of headmasters. They ranged from simple straps to tawses, which were still in use and were therefore kept handily near the bottom. Above them were a succession of canes, increasing in length as they rose up the wall until at the very top there was hung an ancient cat-o'-nine-tails. It was covered in dust and had several of its tails missing: clearly it had long been out of use.

The unfortunate Duncan was hauled into the study on every occasion when he was heard to utter 'wasit', and Mr Potts steadily worked his way upwards through the collection on the wall in an attempt to discover which would prove to be the secret weapon. Alas, the attempt was doomed to failure, for Duncan on account of his habit was as captive to the situation as was Mr Potts on account of his.

Between them they reached at length the top row but one, but here Mr Potts stopped. Whether he thought the ancient cat-o'-nine-tails might not withstand the strain of being used, or whether he doubted that he had the necessary skill, one can only guess. I think the whole experience had aged him; therefore he ducked the issue and instead submitted to the inevitable. Our father was requested to remove Duncan from the school.

To our great relief no further schooling seemed to be planned, and naturally I left also.

Chapter Three

AT THIS POINT OUR parents' marriage came to
an end, since our mother departed. She left
without warning. One morning the Hispano-
Suiza was not in its garage and when it had
not returned by evening we knew at once
what had happened. For days we were devastated, and after our mother's departure
Greenacres was never quite the same. In fact,
the blow was so great that this was when our
childhood ended. We knew instinctively that
now we had to grow up to survive, and that
we would have no other ally, for though our
mother's style was to be distant, none the less
she was all that stood between us and the
unspoken dangers of our expanding world. A
succession of ladies came to keep our father

company, none of whom we liked, and therefore we spent more and more time away from home.

The year was 1937 and Hitler had just walked into Austria. It was also a marvellous year for Clouded Yellow butterflies. That August they came across the Channel in numbers never seen before, and we worked the fields between Ferring and Goring in the pursuit of them, particularly of the rare Pale Clouded Yellows, which were new to us. In this way we reached eventually the boundary of a large estate known throughout the neighbourhood as 'Schwayder's place', where there was a house which could not be seen. It was often talked about in our family and had always retained a mysterious attraction, for nobody knew anything about the house or of the Mr Schwayder who lived there.

We were so excited by the Clouded Yellows that we climbed the estate fence to search for them in the fields on the other side, and since we met nobody we went on collecting for about an hour and a half. Unfortunately, we were so engrossed that we failed to notice the gardener who came up behind us.

In panic we started to make a run for it, only to discover there were further men placed by all the fences and barring our escape. We were seized, our butterfly things were taken from us as though they had been weapons and we were walked at a slow plod until we reached the back door of the large house. There we were locked in a small room, not a single word having been spoken.

Somewhat later we heard a key in the lock and a servant wearing a strange uniform entered. He had a frilly white shirt, tight dark-blue breeches with white stockings and shoes with buckles. In addition to this he had a wig powdered with white. He beckoned us to follow and led us to what was evidently the office of the housekeeper, where seated at a table was a man with cropped grey hair whom we were stood in front of. We had met Mr Schwayder at last.

'Vat ver you doing in my garden?' He had a heavy German accent. 'You are zeeves.'

We looked at each other and prepared ourselves for the inevitable beating. 'We were just exploring,' I said. 'We were catching butterflies, that's why we were there.'

Mr Schwayder looked at me suspiciously. 'I zee. Who is ze uzzer man mit you?'

'He is my brother.'

'Vy does he not speak?'

'He can't. He's dumb.'

'I do not believe your story. I zink you are zeeves.' He paused. 'Vich butterflies?'

'Clouded Yellows and Pale Clouded Yellows.'

'Vere are zey?'

'The man took them.'

Mr Schwayder reached for a small bell which stood on the table and rang it. When another servant in livery entered, he spoke to him in German. The servant left and returned after a while with our butterfly things.

Mr Schwayder carefully examined each article in turn, our nets, the killing bottle and the preserving tin which kept the butterflies from drying. As he did so his manner perceptibly changed.

'I zee you haf Pale Clouded Yellows. Zey are qvite uncommon.'

'And an Adonis Blue,' I said.

He produced a pair of tweezers from his

waistcoat pocket and carefully examined the Adonis Blue.

'Eet is a marvellous insect, unt again not many. Vould you like to zee really rare butter-flies?'

'We certainly would,' I said, sensing that this might signal a reprieve.

He rose from the table and waved us to follow, the man in the peculiar uniform coming behind us. We left the servants' quarters and went into the main part of the house, where we entered a room quite unlike any we had ever seen. White and gold panelling in funny curved shapes stretched from floor to ceiling, and everywhere there were long mirrors so that the room seemed vast. Gold was on everything, even the doorways, where the doors were made of mahogany. It was breathtaking. It was also deserted, for no one seemed to live there besides Mr Schwayder and his servants.

We entered a study in which there were three tall butterfly cabinets made of mahogany, each with two columns of drawers. Mr Schwayder paused, then unlocked one of the cabinets and opened drawers one after another, all packed with rows of Clouded Yellows.

'Zeese are from ze woods near Vienna. Zey are different Clouded Yellows. Ve do not haf zem here.'

We gazed open-mouthed.

'And zis,' continued Mr Schwayder, 'is ze rarest of all. Zis is ze Clouded Yellow variant called Vareefii. You see eet has two black spots on ze left upper wing instead of von.'

I felt Duncan pressing his foot on my heel, then he did so again, which made me look at him. I realised immediately what he meant.

'We have one of those, too,' I said. 'Only ours has two spots on both its upper wings.'

'Zees is not possible but ve vill look. Eet is not possible at all. Zere has never been recorded a double Vareefii.'

The man in uniform was sent to fetch our preserving tin and Duncan opened it, flicking over the contents until he found our prize. Its wings were still open and you could see the two black spots, quite separate, on each upper wing.

Mr Schwayder took out a pair of spectacles and examined the butterfly for at least a minute, his disbelief giving way as a glow of recognition spread across his face.

'But zees eez amazing. Qvite amazing. You are zo lucky. Even in ze great Clouded Yellow year of 1909, in ze whole of ze Vienervald ve only had two Vareefii and zey both vere zingle vuns.'

I felt Duncan catch my heel again. 'My brother Duncan and I would like you to have it, Mr Schwayder. We don't like it especially, and anyway we are still getting the ordinary species for our collection.'

'Do not be zo ridiculous. I could not possibly accept your butterfly,' protested Mr Schwayder.

But after further conversation, much polite hesitation and with mounting excitement, accept it he did.

'I vill write to Heinrich – Heinrich Vaceef, zat eez. Now he lives in Buenos Aires. He vill go mad.' With this Mr Schwayder became so carried away that he danced a little jig.

In due course we were taken, with our gear less one butterfly, back to our railway carriage, and in a Daimler driven by a uniformed chauffeur.

Mr Schwayder waved us goodbye. 'Kom again and zee me and if zere eez anyzing I can do, at any time, you only haf to zay.'

But we were just relieved that it had all turned out so well, and I made no reply.

Chapter Four

GREENACRES HAD BEGUN AS our principal passion, but now its power upon us gradually waned. Partly this was due to the sudden departure of our mother, but it was also connected with the various ladies who appeared as companions for our father who seemed to hold us in resentment. At this time, too, our father changed in his attitude towards us, for while he had always been distant he now became distinctly hostile. He had ceased to concern himself with Duncan since Duncan's illness, possibly because there was no longer any point in his Sunday examinations, while as for myself he ceased even to call me Number Two – in fact, he didn't address me at all. I realised that if he was not very nice to us he probably hadn't been very nice to Mother, either, and that this was probably why she had left. I began to want not to be his son.

And then it suddenly dawned upon me that in all probability I was not his son, anyway. It was because he was not my father that he had no reason to treat with me, now that Mother had left. The realisation struck me with the force of lightning, and what had been confused until then now became as clear as water. Furthermore, I was free. My real father, perhaps, was the racing driver Mother had sometimes told us stories about, whom she called Frank; she had never done that when Father was there.

I never spoke about this to Duncan, and I don't think he ever felt alien as I now did; he had his own way of being free, in his case free of the whole world, not just Father. It was at this point that together we decided to make our future in a different place.

The event that caused our actual departure occurred early one morning the following spring, just after Duncan's sixteenth birthday. We had risen at about six o'clock and gone down our wood looking for a rabbit, but not finding one we were returning to the kitchen for breakfast. Above us were the drawn curtains of our father's bedroom window, and suddenly upon the gable above a large young wood pigeon settled. At once Duncan drew his catapult and let fly.

The bird flew away unscathed and what came down instead was a shower of glass, and a hole appeared in Father's window. Soon it opened and he stood there, still wearing his nightcap. His face was dark with fury and even his black moustache bristled. Then another window opened and from this there leaned, to see what all the fuss was about, a lady with tumbled blond hair. More was to come: the window on the other side of Father opened and another lady appeared, also dishevelled, this one was brunette. They stood there, the three of them, framed by the casements and quite a picture they made. Father's nightcap had a bobble.

'Go away,' he shouted. 'Go away and don't come back.'

'Duncan, that was about your worst miss ever,' I said.

'Wasit,' came the reply, which was one I might have guessed. He started convulsing with laughter and so did I.

When we stopped we looked at each other

and without a word or gesture we knew that the moment had arrived. We went to our railway carriage, found our money-box and counted its contents, which came to two pounds, twelve shillings and eightpence. Next we collected our cooking things, including our Primus stove, and filled our rucksacks with clothes. Duncan fetched his bag of tools, which he strapped on the rear of his bicycle, and more stuff went into my saddle bags. We were used to travelling light, and in half an hour we were ready.

We had never made a plan for this event but we both knew exactly what we were going to do. We were going to London to buy our two-pound tram.

We went through the Downs until we reached the main road to Horsham. It was slow because our bicycles were heavy with their load and we had to walk up the hills, but spring had come early that year and the sun shone. At the end of the day we had got no further than halfway to Horsham, where we found a field and unpacked our things. We were extremely grateful for the sandwiches that Mrs Marrow, our cook, had made for us when we told her we were leaving.

After that we slept on the grass, and the May evening was not at all cold, although London began to seem a long way off.

The next morning we found a workmen's café and spent threepence on buns and coffee. I talked to the lady behind the counter to find out which road to take after Horsham, and she said it was the one that went through Capel to Reigate. She seemed amused that we should want to cycle all that way. 'Why not hitch a lift?' she suggested, adding, 'I'll find you a lorry.'

Thus it came about a short while later that we found ourselves up in the cab with a haulier taking vegetables to Covent Garden market, our bicycles on the back. The driver was chatty, and at first couldn't understand why Duncan didn't answer, until I explained. I told him about our tram, and it ended with him taking us all the way to Acton, which must have been right out of his way. All we had to do after that was to find the depot of the tram company, and now we had all the afternoon in which to do so.

We came upon it in the Uxbridge Road, a great big place with a high roof that you could see a long way off. There were certainly plenty of trams. A long wait followed while Alf, the foreman, was found, but when Alf arrived we had the run of the place. It was a new world and we were entranced.

'What sort of tram was you after exactly?' Alf had a long moustache and whiskers.

Duncan pointed to a tram which had just finished being painted.

'Like that one,' I said.

'That's one of the new T44s, and them's not for sale. I'll show you what is round the back.'

We walked the length of the tramshed and into a yard. It held trams of every description, many decrepit and obviously out of use for a long time, but also there were ones like the picture in the advertisement.

'All these 'ere are two pounds,' said Alf. 'You can 'ave whichever you likes.'

But Duncan had already chosen. He had just climbed up and was sitting in the driver's seat, swinging the big brass operating handle to left and right, polishing it with his sleeve as he did so. He looked transfixed.

'This one will do fine,' I said. 'We'd like it put . . .' We hadn't quite thought it through. '. . . well, next to our railway carriage will be fine. We live at Ferring, which is near Worthing. It's easy to find if you go to Worthing and turn right and we'll be there to show you the place.'

'You 'as to take it from 'ere,' said Alf. 'Right from this back door same as all the other folks. One reason why they been so slow sellin' that not many 'as been taken, I spose.'

We stared at him aghast, and disappointment must have been written on our faces in capitals. It was a matter we had not considered at all, and suddenly the prospect of moving so large an object all the way to Worthing loomed as an impossibility.

'You'd best go away and think about it,' said Alf. 'I'll keep it for you just in case. An' when you 'ave your track and wires laid from 'ere to Worthin' I'll 'ave it waitin' for you.'

It was a terrible blow. We retreated to the churchyard opposite and sat disconsolately on the gravestones. Then we fetched our bicycles and ate the remainder of the sandwiches. All of a sudden we felt tired, so we made a camp and slept there.

Chapter Five

THE NEXT MORNING WE were still asleep when Alf, who must have seen where we went, re-appeared.

'Come and see me when you're up, 'cos I've 'ad an idea of what might suit.'

His coming to see us was unexpected, and certainly our hopes rose a little, but when we joined him in the yard a little later what he showed us was only an old horse-tram. It was a single-decker and had rings for only one horse, for it was quite small. To be honest, it was hardly what we thought of as a tram at all, and Duncan's face was as long as it had been the evening before. It was certainly not what we had come to London for with our two pounds.

However, as we followed Alf round his yard

he showed us how all trams began with horse trams and gradually came to carry more passengers, first at one level, then with an upstairs which had seats beside the 'knife-boards'. His knowledge of trams was endless, and after a while his enthusiasm began to infect us. Therefore, little by little, our view of the matter changed.

The one he had chosen for us was one of the first horse-trams ever built, he explained, even before they had a proper track, so in case it ran out of rails and had to take to the highway it had wheels with solid tyres which could be fixed to it instead.

'We only ever 'ad one of 'em,' he added, 'wot they used to call 'a'penny bumpers back in Queen Vic's time. We got it years ago, when we took over the London–Greenwich line wot built it.' Indeed it had LDGT in large letters on its front.

'But we've still got to get a horse to pull it,' I demurred.

Alf was undismayed. 'I thought o' that, and I'll tell you what to do. Go and talk to the totters – they always 'ave 'orses.'

He had to explain to us who totters were

and where they lived; they went up and down the Uxbridge Road and collected rags and bones.

So next we made the acquaintance of the Acton totters. They were difficult to understand, as half the time they spoke in a language of their own, but they were friendly enough. We were passed from one totter to another, just being told the street they were working where we had to wait until they turned up. It took time but what was soon clear was that there were plenty of horses – there seemed to be a nag with a nosebag at nearly every street corner. The trouble was that they were small animals and didn't look strong enough to pull a tram. As it happened, we knew about such things, because in the past we had been used to take the horses at Miss Marshall's riding stable at Ferring to the forge at Goring to be shod, and we knew exactly what sort of draught a horse could be used for from the ones we saw there.

In the end, we knocked on the door of a hovel in a mews where they told us the totter was giving up. The door was opened by the totter's wife, who related to us in every detail the history of the recent stroke of her unfortunate husband, who had spent most of his days in the coal-heaving trade and had only recently become a rag-and-bone man. We ended up the owners of Homer, a dray horse with a Roman nose, not very tidy to look at but certainly a great deal stronger than most of the horses we had seen.

' 'E's called 'Omer 'cos 'e always tries to turn an' go 'ome, so that's why 'e 'as to 'ave blinkers. 'E's all right if you give 'im a few oats in 'is bag an' as long as Tiger's with 'im,' she informed us.

Tiger was a small black and white dog, evidently not out of the top drawer, and as Homer was so attached to him he was thrown in as part of the deal. Homer and Tiger set us back ten shillings, which was most of our remaining money, but it was a bargain that we never had any cause to regret.

Two days later we were back on the road. It took that time to suit Homer to his new shafts and get his tack sorted out, also to fit the tram's wheels with the tyres. Alf and his mates were true professionals, and perhaps they enjoyed the novelty of the situation, for they also sorted out meals for us at the back of the canteen.

There arose the matter of a destination board. As Alf put it, 'A tram ain't a tram if it 'as nowhere to go to, so it 'as to 'ave one.'

We suggested Horsham, but Alf didn't have any boards for that direction and we finally settled on one for Canterbury. The company had once run trams there, Alf informed us, and once we reached Canterbury we would be halfway to Margate, which was famous for its trams. Clearly Alf had become an important influence in our lives.

'So how do we get to Canterbury and Margate?' I asked, wondering what we were letting ourselves in for.

'Down the Old Kent Road, o' course,' came the answer.

So off we went to find the Old Kent Road.

Our first night stop was at Blackheath, where we found a large common and tied Homer to a tree. He had pulled our tram without complaint and, as the totter's wife had said, his nosebag kept him happy each time we stopped. He showed no signs of wanting to go home to Acton, and we soon found that he went just as well without his blinkers. Tiger also seemed to be happy, though instead of sitting with us on the box he climbed down, evidently preferring to run along beside Homer. Thus we presented ourselves to the world animals first, as it were, perhaps on the principle that where they led we followed.

After we reached the open country beyond Dartford, we were able to make a proper camp and set Homer loose in a paddock. That evening Duncan disappeared with his catapult and returned with a chicken, the feast on which caused an extraordinary change in our view of the world. Although we were in a strange place and far from home, for the first time in our lives we felt absolutely free. We had Homer and our tram to carry us, we had food, just about everything we needed, and suddenly the whole world was right there: all we had to do was seize it, for it was ours for the taking.

Four more days of travel brought us to Harbledown on the outskirts of Canterbury, where the fields gave way to houses whose gardens reached down to the road. It grew dark while we were searching for a camping spot, and in the end we had to settle for a small lay-by where we parked the tram and loosened Homer's harness, leaving him in the rings. We gave him his nosebag and left Tiger sitting in front of him, for all the world like a proprietor. We slept close by under a hedge, hoping that Tiger would alert us if anything was amiss.

In this our hopes were only partly fulfilled, because the next morning we were late getting up and it was half past seven when we scrambled out of the hedge and made our way to the tram. There was no problem with Homer, but to our astonishment the tram was full of people. They sat there on the benches reading their newspapers as though this were the most normal thing, and Tiger was sitting in the front watching them. Then it dawned upon us that we had made a mistake, for where we had parked was not a lay-by at all but a bus stop. There was a sign we hadn't seen which said so.

We were saved from having to decide what to do next by the lady sitting nearest as I entered. 'Third class to Canterbury centre, please,' she said, scarcely looking up.

Duncan nudged me.

'That'll be a penny ha'penny,' I invented.

'Afraid we're out of tickets today. But we'll just remember.'

'It's normally tuppence.'

'Well today is special reductions.'

I saw at once that the coppers would be useful. They meant, for instance, that we might not have to shoot things for our supper every night.

After that I went down the tram and the same thing happened. Everyone knew their fares and usually offered the exact money. No one seemed to mind that there were no tickets, and it was soon clear that our tram was rather popular. People were saying things to each other such as 'Just like it used to be, isn't it?'

Duncan harnessed Homer and then sat on the box holding the reins, and when I had collected the fares I joined him. We held our breath as Homer took the strain of the full tram, but everything held and we moved off smoothly.

We easily recognised the bus stops, and the passengers simply told us when they wanted to get off. There was one hitch when a lady who had been waiting at one of the stops climbed on board. She was a large, important-looking person and she asked for a first-class ticket so I had to explain that we only had third-class. 'Oh no you haven't' she insisted and made me take her double fare. I did not know what to make of this.

The distance to Canterbury was probably only three miles but it seemed longer. What also made it slow were the hills, not proper ones like we had in Sussex but gentle gradients along the course of the road. At one of these the load became too much for Homer and he came to a stop. However, the passengers seemed to be quite used to this happening and simply rose from their seats, got off the tram and walked, at which Homer started to move again. Only the big lady who had paid the first-class fare stayed put.

Tiger also got off and went to have a look at Homer, then, apparently satisfied, trotted along at his side. When at a steeper slope the tram stopped again, Tiger dropped back behind the walkers and started yapping at their heels, and the funny thing was that when they helped by pushing our tram Tiger stopped barking. When downhills had to be negotiated, to relieve Homer I had to act as brakeman, operating a big lever at the front just below Duncan on the box.

In this fashion we reached at length the centre of Canterbury and stopped near the cathedral in a green square, where our passengers disembarked. The big lady was the last to get off and as she did so she asked in a casual way, 'Return down London Road at four o'clock as usual, then?' to which I found myself nodding in reply.

In the respite that followed we spent the morning looking round Canterbury and decided that we liked the place. We liked the cobbled streets and the quaint old cathedral and the people, who seemed relaxed and friendly. Later on they did not all prove to be friendly but that is how they struck us at the time. It all made us think of the Canterbury bells at Greenacres.

In the afternoon I obtained paint and a brush and put 'London Road' in lettering on the other side of the Canterbury sign board. At exactly four o'clock the big lady returned and, evidently glad to find us waiting, she gratefully climbed on board, which seemed a good enough reason to make the return journey to Harbledown. As a matter of fact, this particular person later became such a regular customer of ours that we christened her Big Bertha.

It was during this journey that I realised that there was – there had to be – a strange affinity between Homer and Tiger. It must, I suppose, have been born out of shared experiences, for Tiger seemed always to be aware of his responsibilities as the master of Homer. How this alchemy had come about remained a mystery, but it was clear that Homer depended upon Tiger in a way that he did not upon anyone else, upon ourselves, for instance. In return, Tiger, in his scheme of things, had in Homer a powerful ally in case of need, as we were later to discover.

Chapter Six

IT WAS IN THIS MODEST fashion that we found we had entered the passenger transport business. After this introduction we drove in to Canterbury each morning and out again in the afternoon. We found a place outside the town where we could base ourselves, a paddock at Harbledown, where the lady who owned it let us make a camp and put Homer out to grass on our return.

The journeys became a familiar routine and in the period that followed we truly had the time of our lives. To start with we had a livelihood and beside that a sense of purpose in providing a means for the people of Canterbury to reach their shops, to which they responded by supporting us at every turn. We made a lot of friends.

Obviously they must have realised that we were not a proper transport company but our being unconventional and running an ancient horse-drawn tram was probably what made us so popular. The fact that they only had to wave us down and, wherever it was, Duncan would stop Homer to pick them up added to the attraction. It came to the point that if Duncan had stood as their member of parliament I sometimes thought that they would most likely have elected him.

Our only concern was that we were always taken for a bus, and I constantly had to explain that although we looked like a bus, and behaved like one, we were really a tram, on the lookout for a new set of lines and only on wheels with tyres until we found them.

This distinction, although important to us, seemed to go right over their heads, though to humour us, or perhaps out of politeness, they began to call it 'the tram'.

The only difficulty we encountered was to do with other buses, which we met from time to time when they were working on the same stretch of road. The embarrassing thing was that passengers tended to get off the buses and board our tram instead, and once, when we were going particularly strongly and happened to overtake one of them, I could see from the look on the driver's face that he didn't approve of us, for his mouth was turned down at the corners. However the fares we took enabled us to buy provisions for ourselves and Tiger and oats for Homer. Both seemed quite content with their new circumstances, as were we.

Spring turned into summer and it was then that something happened which caused us concern. One morning we got to the tram to discover that a number of our seat benches had been broken and we had to spend a day repairing them, which was a serious interruption of business. Nevertheless, the incident was forgotten and we resumed our journeys, which grew in popularity in the summer holidays some weeks later when we began to make longer excursions.

But now a much more serious event occurred, one which was to bring about a great change in our circumstances. One evening when we had just completed our journey we were confronted by a gang armed with clubs with which they tried to set about our tram.

Somehow we managed to parry their first attack, partly because Homer, whom I had just taken out of his shafts, reared up and the gang for a moment took fright. It was long enough for Duncan to find his catapult and for me to gather a pile of small stones. The accuracy of the barrage that followed caused them to hesitate, and for a while we succeeded in holding them off, but then the gang's leader sneaked round the back of us and came at me with his knife. I managed to deflect the blow with my hand and the blade struck my other arm, which I only realised when I saw the blood.

He then saw Duncan levelling at him and made a dash towards the rest of the gang, but he was too slow and Duncan got him smack between the eyes. He went out cold on the ground. At this point Homer appeared, with Tiger barking encouragement from behind, and careered about like the clappers, at one moment galloping right through the gang. This made them panic and they made off towards our wood, abandoning the youth on the ground, with Duncan shooting at their backs with relish.

I think we now had the initiative and would have seen them off, but at that moment to our great relief there came riding down the lane a policeman on a bicycle who looked over the hedge, saw the prostrate form, and came over to inspect it. As he did so he saw us and then unfortunately caught sight of Duncan's catapult and the pile of stones.

''Ullo, 'ullo, 'ullo an' what do we 'ave 'ere, then?' he exclaimed.

'We were attacked by a gang,' I said.

'You was attacked by 'im, was yer?' He examined the boy on the ground, who by now was sitting up rubbing his forehead.

''e got me, sir. I was just walking by and 'e got me with 'is bloomin' catapult.'

'There was a whole gang of them attacking us,' I said pointing to the wood to which they had retreated. 'We were trying to defend ourselves.'

But of the gang there was now not a sign.

The policeman took out his notebook and went towards Duncan. 'I am harresting you for 'aving an hoffensive weapon,' he announced, 'an' also causin' grievous bodily 'arm to a passer-by. Which is what I meself saw you was up to.'

Duncan had been shaking in alarm but at

the word 'was' he responded as he ordinarily did.

All that I heard was the word 'shit' and then I knew that we were in real trouble.

'Look 'ere, sonny boy,' said the policeman, 'it's not goin' to 'elp you by your callin' me names and swearin'.' And with that he took out a silver whistle and blew it.

Three police constables arrived, and shortly afterwards an ambulance. They lifted the gang leader, who had managed to faint again, on to a stretcher and put him in the back. I followed, handcuffed to a policeman.

While this was happening Mrs Brown, the lady whose paddock we were in, came over and tried to plead our case with the policemen. However, they were set on their course and her appeals on our behalf were all in vain, although she managed to call to us that she'd look after Homer and Tiger. And so they took Duncan away.

At the hospital the policeman removed my handcuffs and I waited my turn to be stitched up in a row of casualties, some evidently from our fight. Next to me was a boy who had a bad cut that had bled in his hair and down his face. We fell to talking.

'Was you at the bus, too?' I nodded. 'That would have been a really good fight if the coppers 'adn't come and spoiled it. That chap with the catapult he was deadly, an' the bleedin' 'orse – just a pity we had to scarper like that.'

I nodded again.

'Anyway, I suppose you got your ten bob.' He leant across, took my arm and rubbed my wound against his head. 'See, we're blood brothers now. We fight together.'

'But I was on the other side, on the tram,' I said.

'Don't matter,' he said. 'We're blood brothers, that's it.'

It was my initiation. 'What ten bob, then?'

'What we all got, o' course.'

'But who from?'

'We never asks no questions, don't pay yer.' And that was all he would say on the subject before I went in to be stitched up.

Back at the police station they charged me with causing an affray and disturbing the peace, the same as Duncan, although he was also charged with having an offensive weapon. It took me some time to persuade the sergeant at the desk that Duncan's refusal to answer questions was due to his not being able to speak for they had assumed he was just being uncooperative. The sergeant turned back to his notes on Duncan and wrote across the page in large letters, 'Evidently dumb.'

'Right then,' he continued, 'I'd like to see your PSV licence.'

'Our what?' I felt a shudder go through me.

'Your Public Service Vehicle licence.'

'I am afraid we don't have one of those. I mean, we just give people a ride if they want. It's really only for fun.' I could see that the attempt at an explanation wasn't working, for the sergeant wrote down, 'No PSV licence.'

We spent the night locked up in a cell, miserable and quite hungry. They had told us that we would be in court before the magistrate in the morning, and early the next day a rather serious young man came to our cell, explaining that he was counsel on defendants' duty roster and had been allocated to our case. He read out the charge sheet: 'Operating a bus without a

PSV licence.' Just that, nothing about any affray or disturbing the peace.

'If you don't have a licence, you'd best plead guilty,' he added.

I repeated what I had said to the policeman: that we weren't a public service.

He shook his head. 'He'll probably just fine you each a tenner, bind you over and send you on your way. But only if you plead guilty.'

'We haven't got that much money.'

'Then you'll get seven days.'

Duncan showed me what he thought. 'Anyway, we're not pleading guilty to anything,' I said.

He collected his papers with a look of resignation and knocked on the door to be let out.

We were taken to the courtroom and signed to wait in the corridor while the cases in front of us were dealt with. When our turn came we heard the name Scrutton called out and we were ushered into the courtroom. Duncan was led into the dock.

The court clerk got to his feet. 'Your Worship, I had better explain that this defendant is dumb, completely dumb, that is, apart from a few swear words. Therefore may I suggest that Your Worship deals with both this defendant and the next, who is his brother, together. He kind of speaks for both of them.'

The beak looked as if someone had put a dead rat under his nose. 'Very well, then, put up the two of them.'

The charge of operating a public vehicle while not being in possession of a Public Service Vehicle licence was read out, and I pleaded not guilty for us both.

Our counsel got up to make our defence. 'Your Worship, these two young men were certainly not out to commit a felony, and the horse-drawn omnibus they were operating would not be considered a public service in the ordinary sense.'

'I don't see why not,' said the beak. 'It was seen by the constable to have been carrying passengers.'

'Well, if that is the case I suggest that Your Worship deals leniently with the defendants, bearing in mind the infirmity of one of them.'

And that was all he could find to say. Not a word about our being attacked by a gang of hooligans.

The look on the beak's face did not bode at all well. 'That will be for me to decide.'

At that moment there was a stirring in the public gallery and a tall, thin man got to his feet and made his way to the well of the court. When I looked again I noticed the familiar form of Big Bertha beside whom he had been sitting. The man casually handed our counsel a piece of paper and waited while he unfolded and read it. Evidently they came to an understanding.

'Your Worship, there has been a development in the case. May I request a brief adjournment so that it can be considered?'

The beak looked up, paused and then assented. Our case was adjourned, to be heard later in the sitting, and we were taken back to wait in the corridor, ignorant of what the hitch was and by this stage nearly past caring.

Some time later our counsel returned and sat down beside us. 'It is all rather unusual,' he began. 'Mr Beale, a King's Counsel, who happened to be sitting on the press bench, has offered his services for your defence. He says that you have a good case. If you accept, as I would certainly recommend, he will speak when your case returns to be heard.' We nodded. We didn't know what a King's Counsel was but it sounded important.

Eventually we were returned to the dock and Mr Beale got to his feet. He looked impressive now, because he wore a barrister's white tie bands and had on a wig which came halfway down to his shoulders.

He addressed the beak. 'Your Worship, it is my honour to appear before you on behalf of the defendants.'

'Proceed, Mr Beale.' The beak's manner had changed altogether. 'It is not very often that the court comes to be addressed by Counsel in silk.'

'Thank you. First, may I refer Your Worship to Halsbury's *Laws of England*, volume twenty-six, which deals with the Acts concerning public service vehicles.' He held a large book opened at the relevant page, and there was a pause while the clerk of the court searched for the court copy and handed it up to the beak. 'Page 493,' he continued, 'the preamble to the 1919 Act, Public Service Vehicles Licensing. This states that the Act covers all public service vehicles driven by mechanical means, whether petrol, diesel, electric power, batteries, steam or other. The point I am making is that horse-drawn vehicles are not mentioned and therefore by inference are specifically excluded from the cover. It follows that the defendants do not have a case to answer.'

'Perhaps, but there must be earlier Acts which cover horse-drawn vehicles. After all, there were plenty of horse-drawn trams and buses in the previous period.'

'Indeed that is so, Your Worship. As far back as 1863 there were Acts to cover vehicles drawn by horses and even oxen. By 1919 there were a dozen or more such Acts. The point is referred to in the 1919 preamble when it directs that all previous Acts dealing with public service vehicles are by the present instrument made null and void. Presumably, in 1919 they didn't think that horse-drawn buses were any longer relevant. However, there is nothing subsequent that reinstates licences for such vehicles, which I assume to be because the members of parliament who passed this Act hadn't taken account of the possibility of a revival of horse-drawn transport.'

'If so the present case shows them to have been mistaken,' commented the beak.

'I am afraid, Your Worship, that in any society there will always be a few who produce unorthodox solutions to the problem of transport. At least I am relieved to say that oxen were not involved in the present case.'

The beak polished his glasses while considering this unexpected complication.

'Well, dammit, I can't believe that there isn't an Act somewhere that can prevent hooligans from operating like this.'

'My extensive search in Halsbury indicates that there is not, Your Worship, unless you read him differently. It would, of course, be available to you to recommend to the Lord Chancellor a change in the law if you considered that this would be appropriate.'

'Quite so, Mr Beale.' The ball was evidently in the beak's court, and fortunately for us that is where it stayed, because after a suitable pause in which to rescue dignity he finished matters by announcing: 'Case dismissed. Next case, please.'

We were led out of the dock and taken to the back entrance of the court by a distinctly sour-faced police sergeant, who gave us our marching orders.

'You got off this time, thanks to clever Mr Beale,' he said. 'Now I'll give you both a bit of advice. Clear off, right out of this town. There's those 'ere in Canterbury what don't want you 'ere. They'll see to it that our boys nick you next time, if ever they gets 'alf a chance.'

With this we were in no mood to argue.

Chapter Seven

WE WALKED BACK TO Harbledown in silence since our minds were still on the day's events, and it was dusk by the time we reached Mrs Brown's paddock and the refuge of our tram. There a changed scene revealed itself: gone was the chaos we had left when they arrested us, the grass had been cleared of all the debris, and there was Homer quietly grazing in the corner. When we got on board the tram we found the inside completely changed. Everything was immaculately cleaned and the benches all had neatly fitting cushions – in fact, all it needed to be a house on wheels was curtains. The next morning we were still examining this transformation when Mrs Brown came over with Tiger and I told her what had happened.

'I always knew you'd be all right. I mean, to

start with you're well known by now, and what's more you're very popular round here.'

'Not with the law, we're not,' I replied. 'They've really got it in for us.'

'What I also came to say,' she went on, 'is that I've got two sleeping bags for you, as the nights are getting cold and I don't think you should be sleeping under hedges any more. There's another thing. My daughter Heather, she wants to take the fares for you. It's her that's made all the cushions. She's mad on Homer and Tiger, and she's absolutely potty about your tram.'

'I'm afraid we won't be taking passengers any more, Mrs Brown,' I said. 'We're not allowed to and they said if we did they'd put us in prison again.'

At this stage Heather herself appeared, a dark-haired girl of about our age, very bright and breezy.

'They're not doing passengers any more, Heather.'

'Never mind, Mother, leave this to me,' said Heather. Then, turning to us, 'You want someone to look after Homer and Tiger and be dogsbody?'

We looked at each other and then a small

miracle happened. The unexpected appearance of Heather had an effect on Duncan which I had never seen before. Momentarily he looked confused, but then his face lit up and I could see that he was struggling to express something. Suddenly, with what was like a miniature explosion, he came out with a word: 'Hattie'. It was the first proper word he had spoken and evidently it was also an invention of his own. For a moment I thought that his speech was coming back and I was the one who was dumb.

'Seems that's OK by us,' I said when I recovered.

I believe that Duncan was really trying to say 'Heather', but from that moment onwards Hattie was what she stayed.

So it was that we set off next morning, the three of us sitting on the box, the tram looking smarter than it had ever done before, and we presented an entirely new face to the world. Tiger had taken his usual place, which was the left-hand front seat, and Homer seemed to indicate his own satisfaction at the turn of events by taking us spinning along, with Duncan encouraging him at the reins. Hattie, who seemed to have adopted life on the road as readily as her new name, was listening to the portable wireless she had brought with her. Now she wanted to know where we were going.

So single-minded was our urge to get away from Canterbury that this was not a matter that we had yet considered. 'We were going to Margate,' I told her, 'or somewhere with trams and by the sea, but we'll want to find a road that doesn't go through Canterbury. We'll look at the next signpost and then decide.'

However, the decision was made by Homer, because when we came to a fork he turned right, away from Canterbury, and we took the road to Ashford and the south coast. At once we were relieved, for it was true that we were missing the sea, which had always played such a large part in our lives when we lived at Greenacres.

That evening we made a camp fire and Duncan went off and got us a fine rabbit. I skinned it and we made rabbit stew which, together with leaving Canterbury behind, having Hattie as our companion and the prospect of seaside ahead, to raise our spirits considerably.

As for Hattie, she could hardly contain her satisfaction. 'It's the life of a true Romany,' she declared. 'It's in my blood because Granddad was a Romany.' This was quite believable, since her hair was as black as a raven.

It took three days to reach the coast, which was at Bexhill, but we thought it dreary so we turned west towards Eastbourne and the Seven Sisters. We slowed and stopped at each of the seaside places we passed, lounging on the beaches if we liked the look of them and then finding camping places in the Downs behind. At first drifting in this fashion made the days pass easily, for we had enough money to buy what food we needed and the weather was kind.

None the less, the issue of where we were heading refused to go away and as the days passed it became increasingly burdensome, for it became part of the more important matter of what was our larger intention. We were confused until we realised the obvious fact, which was that we were sorely missing our passengers, and the enterprise that they were part of, for without them we had lost something very important: the sense of purpose. But if these doubts lurked in our minds, they certainly did not affect Hattie, who thought that we should simply stay on the road and keep moving on. Yet that didn't seem right to us, either, although quite what we did want we couldn't decide.

By the time we reached Brighton we had begun to sense that there was really one place where we could end up which was our railway carriage at Greenacres. Yet this seemed an admission of failure, and the nearer we got to Worthing the worse we felt about it.

We entered Worthing along the sea-front, reaching East Street by Sayers department store. This at once brought back vivid associations, for it was here that our school uniforms had been bought. Our mother's favourite pastime was to shepherd us to and fro between Sayers and the other big store, Sanders, on Grand Avenue at the other end of the town, and a great deal of our earlier life had been spent marching between those two great competitors in search of Mother's bargains.

Between Sayers and Sanders lay Worthing's two piers, first the new pier, much the longer and always milling with holidaymakers, and then, coming out of West Street, the old pier, which had Worthing's principal ballroom, a fine structure with a green dome at its further end.

The old pier had also been the terminus for the trams. They had stopped running in 1936, but with our new found interest we noticed that both the tracks and the overhead cables still remained.

We lingered and made a night stop where the sea-front ended and gave way to fields.

The next morning we set off again down the long, straight road known as the Ilex Oak Avenue, where we used to gallop the horses on the way back from being shod at the forge. Here we passed the entrance to Mr Schwayder's, and we stopped while I told Hattie about the horses and then related the tale of our adventure there with the butterflies.

The entrance gates were open and, as it happened, a gardener was mowing the verges round the entrance lodge. He must have thought we were tinkers, for he stopped mow-ing and came across to our side of the road to have a closer look at us. We were amazed to discover that it was the same gardener who had caught us in Mr Schwayder's fields, and there was a loud cry of recognition.

'God bless my soul, it's the butterfly catchers,' he exclaimed. 'The Master will surely want to see you. He'll never forgive me if I let you go without his knowing.' With this he sprang up on the box, seized the reins from Duncan, turned into the driveway and drove until we reached the house.

At the news of our arrival a sprightly Mr Schwayder appeared. His enthusiasm was un-diminished, and in no time at all he was talking about butterflies and about Clouded Yellows in particular. He assured us that by now we were famous and the entire world – of butterfly collectors, that is – was talking of the Clouded Yellow that had double black spots. Indeed, as he had once declared that he would, he had written to the butterfly collector in Argentina, Heinrich Vareef, whose reply was in a small black frame on the wall. Evidently it was crucial that Herr Vareef should be clear on one par-ticular detail.

'I looked for all ze fields vere you might haf taken ze Vareefii and zen I bought zem all so zat ze records show eet was Goring Hall.'

Next we had to explain the horse tram and all the rest of the history of the past year, and then he wanted to know where we were going and what were our plans. As it quickly became apparent that in reality there were no plans, he insisted that we should be his guests until such time as we decided. He would be happiness itself if we were to put our tram anywhere on his estate and why not, he suggested, at the spot where we had caught the Clouded Yellows?

This suited us quite well, and since it was now autumn the invitation seemed too good to turn down. Therefore in due course we chose a spot in one of the fields, beside a stream which led down to the sea, as sweet a camping place as ever we found.

Soon we had the run of the whole of Goring Hall. For Hattie it was too good to be true, and in no time at all she made our tram look increasingly like a real home. It received curtains, a galley with a cooker and lights which worked off paraffin and two armchairs, all of which the gardener found for us. Outside were pots of geraniums or whatever else the greenhouse could provide, for Hattie always had an eye for detail. Soon she became our ambassador in all the departments of Mr Schwayder's house, and, since that remarkable palace was inhabited solely by an elderly bachelor, she provided it with a womanly touch which it had probably never had, arranging flowers in the principal rooms and adding her own gaiety everywhere. Mr Schwayder was quite captivated. Each day he came to visit us, partly, I think, to make sure that we were still there.

For our part, with time on our hands we started making expeditions again. It was lucky that we carried our bicycles in the tram's storage, for we ventured far afield and rediscovered favourite places such as Swanbourne Lake at Arundel. Here there were slopes of beech trees and a lake below in which we swam, where the water ran down like crystal twenty or thirty feet to the chalk. We went to Greenacres to see Mrs Marrow and brought back with us the remaining contents of our workshop, but Greenacres didn't seem like home any more.

We had music from Hattie's wireless and, of course, the news, at that moment mostly about Hitler and where he was going into next. When winter came Hattie began to learn our sign language, which at first she found extremely strange, since our hands moved so rapidly that she couldn't watch them and take in all the other gestures happening at the same time. But she persevered and after a couple of months she began to grasp it so that for the first time she and Duncan were able to communicate without me. I think that it was at about then that she started to become attached to him. Besides being good-looking, Duncan had a very mature appearance which had always attracted girls, and his silence made him seem masterful. The fact that he scarcely took any notice of them made them all the keener, and Hattie was no exception. What Hattie did not know, and I only slowly realised myself, was that his illness had left its mark on this part of Duncan's makeup. I think that he did not respond to girls in the way that, for instance, I did.

For me there was a curious irony in all this, since I believed that it was myself and not Duncan who had been the first object of Hattie's affections. The reason for my saying so was an incident which had occurred some time earlier. Hattie was cleaning and I was busy painting inside the tram, although my thoughts were elsewhere, when suddenly and unexpectedly I found Hattie's face close to my own, her eyes half closed. My heart began to race as it dawned upon me that she was inviting me to kiss her. But a wave of shyness overcame me, I became just an awkward teenager and, terrible to relate, I let the moment pass. In a second she had turned away and, sad to say, I never saw that lovely upturned gypsy face again.

Chapter Eight

IN THE SPRING THERE was a new craze which we picked up from the wireless. We strutted it round the gardens, the three of us, arms linked, time and again:

'Everything free and easy, now we are bright and breezy, this way, that way, any way at all, you'll find us all doing the Lambeth Walk.'

The mood was light-hearted, but for Duncan it did not stay that way, for we had not been at Goring Hall long when he began to draw more and more into himself and a dark cloud seemed to come over him. Everyone became aware of it, especially Mr Schwayder, and he and Hattie became more than usually attentive, almost like nurses. They thought it due to depression of his spirits, but to me it did not seem to be that at all, more that he was beset by doubt of some sort, some conundrum that he was unable to solve. Day after day he brooded, as though searching for a solution which he was never able to find.

Mr Schwayder came to visit us every day, and on one occasion appeared particularly concerned when he beheld the dejected Duncan. He teased him, he pretended that if Duncan was miserable he himself would be miserable as well.

'Vatever you vish I vill give to you to make you yourself again.' He repeated this several times as he talked, and I really think he must have meant it.

But Duncan had to find his own way out of his difficulties and in this he presently succeeded, or at least it would be truer to say that a solution was otherwise found which proved to be a very strange one indeed.

It happened during Mr Schwayder's visit one morning. Duncan had looked like a dormouse half asleep in a corner, but now he suddenly got to his feet and with impression of enormous effort, the like of which had not happened since he had said 'Hattie' at Canterbury, he came out with another word. For all the world it sounded like 'Popadom'. This strange new word coming from Duncan left us in a state of shock.

Mr Schwayder recovered first. 'Popadom. Yez, of course, Popadom,' he said shaking his head sagely.

But I am sure that neither he nor we knew what to make of it.

Nothing happened for three or four days, but then a smart delivery van bumped its way across the field, followed in the distance by Mr Schwayder. From it two men in dark-green uniforms with peak caps got out and proceeded to carry on to the tram box after box of what were evidently popadoms until they were piled so high on the benches that you couldn't see out of the windows.

At this point in the proceedings Duncan came striding in from the wood with a couple of rabbits slung from his belt. He paused at the doorway, his brow knitting as he took in the scene, and then he let out a mighty roar and with that he leapt among the boxes, pounding them to pieces with his fists and hurling them in every direction. It was such a rage as I had only witnessed once or twice in the whole of Duncan's life.

One of the boxes struck poor Mr Schwayder in the neck and burst over his shoulders, covering him from head to foot with pieces of popadom. He raised his arms in the air as if in supplication, and then, as fast as his rather short legs could carry him, he ran away across the field.

When the storm abated, even as quickly as it had arisen, a troubled silence descended and for that day and the next we lived in a sort of limbo for we were sure we would be asked to leave. Poor Mr Schwayder must in his dismay have been deeply affronted, we thought, and what on earth must the staff be thinking of it all? The least I could do was to make my apology to Mr Schwayder for the unhappiness that Duncan's strange behaviour must have caused him, and I decided to do this on my own. So I went to the house to look for him and found him sitting in a small room surrounded by Hattie's flowers.

I was immediately filled with embarrassment, because at the sight of me he started to cry.

'Alvays I vaz successful in my life,' he sobbed. 'Zo many zings I haf done vich I knew vould make people happy. And for Duncan I vanted so much to make him happy, but all zat I haf done ees to make him go crazy. Zat is vat makes me cry.'

And with that he started to weep so pitifully that I began to wonder whether this was quite the normal thing for a Viennese person.

For a while I could think of nothing to say that would not make matters worse. Of course, I was aware by now of what had been in Duncan's mind and what he had been trying to say, for clearly 'popadom' was absurd and far from what he wanted.

I eventually plucked up my courage. 'I am afraid that Duncan made a terrible mistake. He got the word all wrong. He didn't mean popadom at all.'

'Vat did he mean, zen? Tell me.'

'He meant "proper tram".'

He considered this for a minute or so. 'But he already has a proper tram.'

'Well, actually, we only got the horse tram more or less by mistake.'

I explained what had happened and how Alf had shown us every tram in the depot at Acton and the horse tram was the only one we could manage to take away. I told him how Duncan had sat polishing the driving handle of a splendid tram which was just like the one in the advertisement for the two-pound tram. I took out the picture from my wallet where I kept it and showed it to him.

'Zat vas ze one zat Duncan really vanted?' By now Mr Schwayder was recovering and looked quite relieved. 'I zee everyzing. Now I zee vy he vas so mad. Eeet is truly terrible for him not to be able to tell us vat is in his mind, terrible.'

'Well it is, but we are used to it. The trouble is that when he does say a word, which is not very often, he doesn't always get it right. For instance, he called Heather Hattie.'

There was further conversation but to my great relief there was no talk of our having to depart, and in due course I hurried to relay this good news to the others.

Next day I returned and sought out Mr Schwayder, who seemed by this time to have regained his natural state of mind. 'I haf zought for a long time about ze tram,' he began as I entered. 'You know zere used to be trams vich ran all ze vay along ze front at Vorthing, starting from ze old pier.'

'I know,' I said. 'I remember them.'

'Ze old pier vas ze terminus for ze trams but zere vas alzo ze ballroom. Ven trams vere given up and zere vas talk about pulling down ze pier, I zought it vas a great pity zat Vorthing people should lose zere ballroom, so I took zteps to see zat zey didn't. I bought ze pier and zo it is zere today, alzough I never zought zere would ever be trams zere again. Now I zink zat perhaps I vas mistaken.'

'How do you mean, mistaken?'

'Vell, how do you zink Duncan vould like it if I got ze tram he liked so much and put it on ze pier?'

'I think he would like it very much indeed,' I said. 'So would Hattie and so would I.'

Some days later I found myself in the back of Mr Schwayder's blue Daimler on my way to Acton in search of a new tram. The journey took place in silence on account of the glass partition separating the front from the back, which for some reason the chauffeur insisted on keeping closed. When we reached the tram depot we drove round it until I spotted Alf. The expression on his face when the chauffeur opened the door and I stepped out is something I shall remember as long as I live.

'My, we 'ave come up in the world,' he exclaimed, surveying the Daimler. 'But then I always knew you was serious, you two. An' now I suppose you're goin' to tell me you'll be running a tram service, in which case you may as well 'ave the lot, since none's gone since you 'ad the 'orse tram.'

'Thank you, Alf, but one will do,' I replied. 'It's just that my brother Duncan doesn't seem able to live without a proper tram.'

'Your brother wot doesn't talk?'

'That's the one,' I said.

He led the way across the yard and we climbed aboard the tram in which Duncan had sat at the controls. There followed a long lecture from Alf on what was required to put it into proper order. The engine needed to be stripped down and the emergency batteries given new plates. Out of politeness I patiently took note of all these details, although it was certainly not anyone's intention that the tram should actually run, or so I thought. Finally he found the work manual, which showed that the tram had been commissioned in 1926, and I left clutching this and a picture of the tram as it had first appeared in the papers.

Some weeks later the tram, our proper two-pound tram, was to be seen moving along the sea-front at Worthing on board a low-loader, from which it was hoisted on to the tram rails of the old pier to the astonishment of passers-by. It looked happy to be home, this symbol of past and better times. Then of course everything had to be explained to Duncan but that I left to Mr Schwayder.

Chapter Nine

WE CONTINUED TO LIVE in what we now called the old tram in Mr Schwayder's field, not least for the sake of Homer and Tiger, but each morning we cycled to the old pier to spend the day there, for a new chapter had opened. We all had our jobs to do.

The tram's interior was the province of Hattie, who had her own ideas, and to intervene was more than we dared. Meanwhile, Duncan, who, following his seizure of rage, had miraculously recovered his old composure, seized upon the work manuals and set about stripping down the engine and the electric system. Indeed, such was his enthusiam that I began to wonder whether he intended that the tram should actually run, although to me this seemed wishful thinking. It was true that the old rails and overhead cables still existed, but obviously there was no electric current in them and we could never run the tram for any distance on its batteries alone. But Duncan worked away so purposefully that it was clear that such considerations did not enter his mind, and after the first time that I raised the matter I decided not to do so again.

My job was to repair the outside of the tram, in particular to repaint the signs, for it was covered with cheerful advertisements, pictures painted directly on to the metalwork, giving it a character all its own. There were advertisements for Ovaltine in a steaming cup, for Cerebos salt with a child pouring salt over a chicken as it ran, next to Oakey's glasspaper in large capitals and of course for Bisto with the Bisto kids. My favourite, though, was 'My Goodness my Guinness', with a picture of an ostrich in a zoo which had swallowed the keeper's glass of beer.

That autumn came the news that Hitler was on the march again, and Mr Chamberlain had to fly to Munich to persuade him to stop. When he returned he spoke on the wireless and said it would be peace, not war, after all. The terrible moment seemed to have passed.

Just before Christmas the tram was finished,

and by then neither of us doubted that we were going to test it, especially as Hattie had soon to leave to be with her mother at Canterbury. The engine was completely reassembled and we had virtually new batteries, which the manual said would run the tram for a distance of three to four hundred yards on the level if driven at slow speed. Next we had to turn our attention to the rail system. Turning loops had been constructed in the centre of Worthing and at either end of the tram system but a reversing loop at the old pier had to be rebuilt and the points which had become corroded by the salt had to be freed. The running plan was easy to see, for the loop had been made with points at both entry and exit so that the tram could be turned about for the next journey outward.

When everything was ready, Duncan insisted on attaching the tram's conductor-arm to the overhead cable, although of course this carried no current, because in his view it balanced the tram properly and, besides, the tram had to be complete in every detail.

For our trial run we decided to go as far as the shops on Grand Avenue, which were lit with Christmas decorations. The brightest, standing out in the fading light of the afternoon, was Sanders store, outside which a banner hung across the road proclaiming: 'Sanders wishes a merry Christmas to you all' in coloured lights. This seemed to be a good point to aim at.

We moved off to an impressive start as Duncan pulled the tram's bell, which sounded like a high-pitched clock rapidly striking two. There was a general clanking of iron wheels on the tramway, and had there been onlookers they would have taken us for one of the ordinary working trams they had once been used to.

However, since we were on battery power we moved extremely slowly and it was some time before we managed to cover the distance to Sanders store. When we got there we saw that the illuminated banner actually rested on our overhead cables, so, even had we planned to do so, we could not have gone any further, though in any case we were at the limit of where the batteries were able to carry us.

At this point, with Sanders just ahead of us, we drew to a standstill and savoured the moment in a glow of satisfaction at how well our tram had performed. It had done better than we could ever have imagined and Duncan, with his legs up on the next seat, was beside himself with joy. Hattie was even more jubilant than we were, realising for the first time that the tram had a future, and more particularly, a future for her as well as for us.

It was then that we became aware that the tram was gently moving and we abruptly realised that the road had a tiny forward slope. Duncan sprang to his feet and seized the hand-brake and I rushed outside to find blocks or anything to put in front of the bogies to arrest our slide, but neither the brake nor the blocks succeeded in arresting the tram, and to our despair all our efforts were in vain. It drifted, picking up speed until the conductor-arm struck the greetings sign and became entangled with it, and then gradually we came to a halt.

We got the tram's emergency ladder and climbed up to see what could be done. For some time we wrestled with the conductor-arm but all the wires were under considerable tension and it became clear that something would have to be cut. I fetched our tools and with the greatest care we worked for about ten minutes, at which point, much to our relief, we seemed to be free, and so Duncan returned to the controls. Very slowly he inched the tram backwards, and at first all seemed to be well, but then as we moved further the whole central section of the banner came away and fell in a heap in the road. The rest of it stayed up, although it sagged in the middle, then slowly the two halves slid together and the whole banner appeared to undergo a sea change because the greeting now read 'Sander you all'. We knew not what to do.

For a few minutes it remained brightly lit, but a short circuit must have developed for next there was a terrible bang and the lights went out – unfortunately, not just in the sign but in the whole of Sanders as well. It might have been a blackout rehearsal. In a short while it seemed that the entire Sanders staff came out and lined the pavement, staring in amazement at ourselves and the tram, which had begun to move again, although agonisingly slowly, since the batteries were nearly finished. We waved to them and they waved to us; indeed, a number of them accompanied us all the way back to the old pier, cheering when we came to a halt and doing so even louder when we started up again. It was not at all what we wanted, because even when we got to the pier they were there,

which left us nowhere to hide our embarrassment.

It was quite amicable as far as it went, but I did
not think that this would be the end of the
matter, nor was it.

The next day we still thought it might blow
over, since at first nothing happened. But
when we got the local newspaper we found
that it had on its front page a picture, taken by
a photographer who had happened to be
passing, showing the Sanders greetings sign
with its shortened, and now frankly insulting,
message. This, as we quickly realised, was not
going to make us popular with Sanders. At
this point we almost made up our minds to
scarper, but Hattie ordered that we should
remain. 'Stay and face the music' was what she
said.

Then one of the Sanders doormen arrived.
We were to accompany him, otherwise, he said,
a policeman would be sent for and would
probably arrest us. We were driven to Sanders
and taken to a basement room marked 'Security', where he handed us over to another man
who looked a proper bruiser, and he started

asking us a lot of questions. I tried to explain that we hadn't intended to get caught up in the greetings sign and it was due to there being a slope which we hadn't noticed. Then he started to go for Duncan, perhaps because he looked older, until I explained that there was no point, since Duncan couldn't speak. At least this time Duncan stayed silent.

As it went on the man began to look more and more puzzled and in the end he ran out of questions and handed us on to a higher-up official who asked much the same questions and then tried to make us admit that we had been attempting to sabotage the banner. He even suggested that we were employed by Sayers, the store at the other end of the town. After this he went away and left us with the security man, who now said nothing. Eventually a woman, whom we took to be a secretary, came and we were taken in the lift again, this time to the top floor where she knocked on a door which said 'T. Parker, Chairman'.

It was certainly him we now found ourselves standing in front of, there could be no mistaking that. His jaw jutted forward in a determined way, and to put it mildly he did not look at all friendly.

'I have only one question to ask you and I would strongly advise you to answer it,' he said curtly without looking up from the papers on his desk. 'I want to know who you are working for. I assure you that you will gain nothing by hiding it, because I have a strong suspicion that I already know. Therefore I do not choose to waste my time.'

'We aren't working for anyone,' I replied. 'In fact, we aren't working at all.'

'Let me express myself differently. A tram has damaged my property. Who is the owner of the tram?'

'It's our tram,' I replied, 'and I'm terribly sorry about your property. It's just that we had a brake failure and there's a slope in the road, as you can see.'

'What I can see is that you are being extremely uncooperative, so what sort of fool do you take me for? My enemies I can deal with, provided I know who they are and that I have ample means to find out. I repeat, what is the company running this tram?'

'There isn't one. We own it.'

'Don't think you can hoodwink me. How could two . . . two . . .'

'I promise you we do own the tram. I'm terribly sorry about the damage, and I am certain we can mend your banner and make it light up again.'

He was glaring at us and I thought that at any minute he would start waving his arms at us or worse.

'You see, we were given it by Mr Schwayder.'

He hesitated. 'Mr Schwayder who lives at Goring Hall?'

'That's right. It was to replace our horse tram, which was rather old and Homer − that's our horse − was getting tired of pulling it.'

'For the life of me I can't see why Mr Schwayder should give you a tram.'

'Well, actually, it was because Duncan had given him a Clouded Yellow.'

'And what on earth is that?'

'A Clouded Yellow butterfly. Not an ordinary Clouded Yellow, but a Vareefii variant.'

'A what?'

'A Vareefii has two black spots instead of one,

only ours had two on each of its front wings, and that's especially rare. Duncan gave it to him because Mr Schwayder's a very important collector.'

'Let me get this quite straight. What you're telling me is that you gave Mr Schwayder a butterfly and in return he gave you a tram. This takes a bit of understanding, I must say.'

I could feel Duncan pressing my arm so I realised that I had better go on talking. 'He was so pleased he even bought the field where we caught the Clouded Yellow so that he could say it was on his own property when he wrote to tell his friend Heinrich about it.'

'Heinrich?'

'Heinrich Vareef, in Argentina. The man who discovered the butterfly with those spots. That way it would get into the record books that it was caught at Goring Hall.'

'Heinrich Vareef . . . in Argentina,' he repeated slowly.

Mr Parker's eyes had been getting steadily wider and his jaw fell so that it almost touched his chest. At this moment there was a knock on the door and the secretary came in.

'Miss . . .' Mr Parker began, but his voice trailed off.

'Moneypenny,' she said, smart as lightning. 'Excuse me, but your next appointment is overdue, Mr Parker. I thought I had better tell you'.

'Ah . . . thank you . . . thank you, Miss Moneypenny. And now please be so kind as to show these two gentlemen out. And perhaps you would take them to the canteen and make sure they get a proper luncheon.'

Miss Moneypenny ushered us out and down to the basement once more, and there we did indeed get given our dinner, or rather our luncheon.

We returned to our pier wondering what would happen next, but two days later we were summoned back to the office of Mr Parker. He appeared to have recovered his bark.

'I have considered the matter of the tram and of your predicament at some length and, although I still regard you as trouble-makers, I am prepared to offer you a means by which you can settle your liability for the damage to my store.

'In general, I favour the idea of a tram running on the old tramway and since this also seems to have been what you were attempting I have decided that, on certain conditions, I can extend to the project a limited support.

'The first condition is that the entire venture is placed under my direction and control. Secondly, your tram would have to carry advertisements for my store in place of those that you are carrying at the moment. These I would have prepared.

'I realise,' he continued, 'that this would mean you would lose the revenue from your current advertisers. However, I would make this loss good.'

'We don't actually get anything for them at the moment,' I said.

'I see. If that is the case then you are more du—' He stopped. 'I mean, more stupid than I thought. In any case, I would make the potential loss good.'

It was our turn to stare.

'Oh, and there is another thing. When you reach the further end of the tramway I wish you to turn in front of Sayers department store so that they have a good view of my advertise-

ments. That is a summary of what I am propos-
ing: have you any objections?'

'None, Mr Parker, none at all,' I replied. I
didn't need to consult Duncan: he was chuck-
ling.

Chapter Ten

AFTER CHRISTMAS WE were summoned again, but this time it was to discuss practical details and there were certainly plenty of these which we had not even considered. As well as a driver's licence, Duncan would require what was called a Tramway Familiarity Certificate. Furthermore Duncan, who was actually eighteen, had to be at least twenty-five to qualify for the licence, but here we decided to rely on his appearance since the fact was that with his greying hair he looked about thirty. Just to be on the safe side, we altered the date on his birth certificate with the help of a little ink eradicator.

The whole process was more complicated than we could have imagined but in Mr Parker we quickly found we had an ally as firm as a rock. He was a town councillor and knew all the levers to pull, and so keen did he become on the project that one by one he pulled them. For instance, the provisional licence that Duncan received required him to be accompanied by a tram driver of five or more years' experience, although this would have been impossible because there was no tram driver who still lived in Sussex. The authorities were prevailed upon so that this rule was waived.

It was then we realised that Mr Parker was just as enthusiastic about trams as we were. At times he came to watch Duncan driving, and when Duncan swung the big brass arm I saw that Mr Parker would have been happy to have exchanged places with him. His face bore a smile, and his head swayed gently from side to side as though he was inwardly cheering Duncan on, which the assistants who were with him copied so that, as I looked at their faces, I came to think that we had brought a little happiness to Sanders store.

At about this time it happened that Mr Parker and ourselves reached agreement on a rather different matter. One day we were talking when, out of the blue, an altogether new subject came up.

'Has it ever occurred to the pair of you that you might profit by staying on the right side of the law?' he asked casually.

'No,' I said. 'You can't do that. I mean, whatever side you are on the law is on the other side and there's nothing you can do about it.'

'That's not the way I see it,' said Mr Parker. 'How do you think I could run a business like mine and be on the wrong side of the law?'

I saw what he meant and I was sure that there was an answer to it, but at the time I couldn't find it.

'May I suggest, entirely as an experiment but one in which you would have my assistance, that you try conducting your affairs as I do mine, according to the laws of the land. Have you ever considered that possibility?'

'Well, no,' I said. 'But I suppose we could give it a try.' Duncan looked completely blank.

It was March before anything happened to the tramway, but then an army of workmen descended upon it and the whole system was overhauled. After that events moved fast – we got our 'provisional' and an electricity supply which enabled us to practise short journeys. Duncan seemed rejuvenated and Hattie, whose heart was set on carrying passengers, looked as smart in her uniform as our tram itself. Furthermore, she now proved herself as valuable an ambassador where Mr Parker was concerned as she had been with Mr Schwayder. Actually, we did already possess one passenger. This was Tiger, who took the same seat, the one on the left behind the driver, as he had in our horse tram.

By now we had a new and splendid livery in crimson and cream, courtesy of Sanders workshop, together with a series of features advertising Sanders which covered the tram, front, back and sides. Thus attired we ventured to the further parts of the tramway system, testing the turning loops, including that which had been newly laid in front of Sayers store. On those first trips it soon became clear that our tram was popular with the people of Worthing, for whenever we stopped crowds would gather as if it was an event, and if the tram didn't turn their heads Hattie certainly did. Our most adventurous foray was to the barracks at the eastern end of the town where on our first visit a strange incident occurred. The sight of the tram must have cast such a spell over the sergeant drilling some men on the square that he forgot to give the order to about-turn. In consequence of this, the squad continued until it reached the cliff top and then disappeared over it, with the exception of a single recruit who, when the order was finally given, turned smartly and marched back to the square on his own.

Soon after this Duncan passed his driver's test.

Mr Parker had arranged that the tramway should be officially opened and this was set for 13 August, which was the day of the annual Mayor's Procession. By custom on this date the mayor and aldermen, wearing ceremonial dress and badges of office, walked through the streets of the town like a royal progress. For this ceremony our tram was chosen, partly because the mayor was no longer capable of walking the distance. It was arranged, since the mayor's residence was close to Grand Avenue, that a reception would be held in the ballroom of the old pier, after which our tram would convey the mayoral party to the junction at North Street, where they would get down and then walk the short distance to the town hall, at the same time signifying that the tramway was thus opened and ready for public use.

Many days were spent in preparing our tram for this important event. Uniforms were made, brass gleamed and all the seats were recovered by Hattie, that for the mayor having a pattern in gold braid on its back.

On 13 August the ceremony duly took place. The local press appeared in force, and while the reception was taking place inside the ballroom we had to endure the cameramen, who took all manner of pictures of the tram and ourselves, self-conscious in our uniforms and in the outcome looking somewhat sheepish. The exception was Hattie, photographs of whom in her own new uniform complete with pill-box hat, all of Hattie's own creation and her mother's handiwork, made the front pages of every local newspaper, including even the *Brighton Herald*.

When the reception at the pier was over the mayor and his party climbed aboard the tram. There was one small hitch when Tiger, believing it to be his, refused to give up the mayor's seat. Much to the mayor's credit, Tiger remained while he took the next best seat behind.

After this the seven aldermen and a large number of town officials were steered to their seats by Hattie, and those for whom she could not find space went upstairs. To our surprise one of the aldermen proved to be none other than Mr Schwayder, who in this capacity was able to discover that the tram he had provided was fully functional, was indeed a proper tram.

We started the engine and with grinding and clanking the tram backed into its turning loop, a manoeuvre judged by Duncan to be suitably impressive. We then made our way down West Street and turned into North Street, where a crowd had gathered at the tram stop to watch the mayor and his party descend. Thereafter it took some minutes for the procession to re-form, and when it had done so we were some-what surprised to find that Tiger had taken up position as its rear marker and remained there as the party marched to the Town Hall. Possibly this was because on leaving the tram the mayor had warmly shaken each of us by the hand, therefore perhaps Tiger thought that doing as he did was no more than an extension of good manners, or else he just wanted to make up for having not moved over. Be that as it may, his mission completed and someone having hung a gold chain about his neck, he returned at a dignified trot to the tram and ourselves amid much acclaim from the crowd, the white parts of his coat agleam in the sunlight.

Not surprisingly this secured for Tiger his own photograph on the front pages.

Chapter Eleven

IT WAS A SENSATIONAL start, and in the sunny days that followed we rode high in the expectation that our new way of life would lead far into the future, bringing us happiness and wealth and even a degree of fame. Unfortunately, fate had something else in store. The sunny days we counted were just twenty-one in number and then abruptly they stopped, because on 3 September, as no one really expected, the war started.

At first things went on as before, but that was only on the surface, for from that moment a whole world disappeared and a scene of gaiety was replaced by one of fear and foreboding. Our own lightness of heart vanished and the peacetime we had just left behind soon began to seem like a childhood memory. It is not too much to say that on that day youth ended and the bottom of our world fell out.

As we changed, Worthing did so even faster, for in place of being a seaside resort for holiday-makers it became part of the front line of war. Beach huts were replaced by pillboxes as the military arrived and spread themselves along the sea-front. We lost most of our new passengers, because only the locals now remained, although we soon had soldiers from the barracks of the West Sussex Fusiliers, which doubled and then trebled in size. It was not long before this Eastern run, as we called it, became our main business, since we formed the link between the soldiery and the town, starting early and finishing late. Duncan in particular seemed fired by a new patriotism and took our new wartime role very seriously, deciding that we should carry all passengers in uniform at half price.

We joined the Local Defence Volunteers, believing that in the LDV we would find our-selves in uniform practising with rifles and de-fending the Downs. Indeed, it did start that way, though the rifles they gave us were wooden ones and all we learned was drill. Our drill instructor was a certain Sergeant Breakspear, evidently a veteran of the last war or possibly of the one before that, and it makes me sad to relate that from the start he took against Duncan.

The reason for this was his drill performance. As I may have mentioned, Duncan suffered from being left-handed, which condition seemed also to affect his feet, with the result that when Sergeant Breakspear gave the command 'Left turn', for instance, Duncan would be just as likely to turn right. 'By the left, quick march' was often similarly misinterpreted.

Matters came to a head as soon as we started to learn arms drill, and I am sorry to say that quite early on in the proceedings Duncan made a dreadful mistake. On the command 'Slope arms', his rifle ended up not on his left shoulder like the rest of us but on his right.

It was too much for Sergeant Breakspear, who appeared to burst into a sweat. There was a pause, followed by the command 'Left-handed volunteer one pace forward'. Nothing happened. 'Yes, you,' he yelled, pointing at Duncan, who then had to step forward.

'Quick march,' the sergeant continued. Beside the cricket pitch which served as our parade ground were benches provided for the spectators, and Duncan's march continued until he reached one of these. There came the further command 'Volunteer, halt,' and then 'Volunteer, dismiss.'

'An' leave your bleedin' rifle on the bench,' Sergeant Breakspear roared.

As soon as the parade finished I made my way over to find Duncan, who in his exclusion sat disconsolately on a fallen tree on the edge of the wood. He looked the picture of misery; but then I noticed that he was holding a hare, which he must have bagged in the wood, and I knew he was all right.

After we got back to the tram Hattie roasted the better parts and when she started to laugh as the story came out, we both began to laugh as well.

Unfortunately, following this incident it was decreed that we should be transferred to Air Raid Precautions, where we were made responsible for gas-mask drill and blackout inspections. Worse still, we lost our LDV uniforms, receiving only ARP armbands, and after that all our time was spent checking that people's blackout curtains had no chinks. Furthermore, although we lived in West Worthing, we were assigned to beats in East Worthing, while the volunteers from there inspected in our own locality. Not, in our opinion, very efficiently, either; for instance, although the side windows of the ballroom on the old pier were blacked out, the large skylight, out of sight from the pier but visible to us from the upstairs of the tram, was always ablaze with light.

The Saturday-night dances there continued, and this meant that we had to drive most journeys under blackout conditions with dimmed headlights and blinds down. Not all the journeys were peaceable and we eventually had to provide Hattie, not that she wasn't capable of giving as good as she got, with a volunteer minder from the camp.

Our favourite minder was Rifleman Kelly, whose enthusiasm for trams was as great as any of ours. Kelly was a natural leader of men, and a word from him seemed to be all that was required to subdue drunken and otherwise difficult Saturday-night customers. The reason for this, as we shortly discovered, was that he was also, or rather had been, the regimental sergeant-major, now reduced to the ranks on account of a certain unfortunate incident. This was losing most of his drill squad over the barrack square cliff prompted by our first run on East Street.

'I don't know why there was so much fuss, 'cos they was all OK,' he explained, 'all except Private 'Iggins, who broke 'is leg, but 'e was always one for getting hisself into trouble, if he could find any to get into.'

Altogether, Rifleman Kelly was a useful acquisition. There was, for instance, the occasion of the yearly football match between East Worthing and West Worthing in the West Sussex league. You would have thought that in a time of war not a great deal might separate the loyalties of these two sides, but this would ignore the fact that the East Worthing team and its supporters were largely drawn from Sayers department store, while those of West Worthing came from Sanders. Unfortunately, this year's game had concluded in a draw and the supporters chose our tram as the scene on which to continue the game to a conclusion. This ended, however, when Rifleman Kelly appeared, accompanied by a number of fusiliers of impressive size who set about the football fans, driving them not only off our tram but all the way back to their lodgings in the town, and never after that under Rifleman Kelly's watchful eye did we get any more fights.

Our life had changed and we were now fully occupied. We had to give up spending Saturday and Sunday nights in the old tram at Goring Hall and only went there on weekdays, mainly for the sake of Homer but also to get our supply of rabbits and the odd chicken. The rest of the time we lived where we worked. Except, that is, for Hattie, who had just come into a legacy of five hundred pounds from her aunt, and with it had bought herself a house, one of the last new developments just where the sea-road ended. The sale notice, the cause of this excitement, had said three hundred and ninety-five pounds, so Hattie still had something over and by now she had moved in, together with a lot of the geraniums. It was, all were agreed, more suitable.

In the run-up to Christmas we had air-raid warnings, which we knew from being wardens in the ARP were mostly practice affairs, although there were some hit-and-run raiders. But at about this time someone decided that Hitler needed a Christmas present, and a bomber actually succeeded in dropping a bomb on Berlin. As a result of this, raids on England were begun and the throbbing of German aeroplanes became an all too familiar sound. The West Worthing siren was sited on the sea-front next to a unit of sound detectors less than a hundred yards away from us, and when it started wailing we had of course to turn out for our ARP duty.

Occasional bombs were dropped around us, not so much on targets as simply jettisoned by German bombers when they were chased off by the night fighters. Once we had a grandstand view of this, when a German bomber was picked up in the searchlights as it crossed the coast and then headed home with every anti-aircraft gun in Worthing blazing up at it. Its bombs just missed the Hove road and fell into the sea with muffled thuds.

At about this time we made the acquaintance of Eddie March. What was the equivalent of a small lighthouse was erected at the end of our pier on the sea side of the ballroom. It consisted of a single fixed light mounted over a small control room and in addition had, for reasons which were not clear, a substantial hoist for raising loads from the pier end. It was all completed in what seemed to be a hurry, and when it was finished Mr March had arrived to man it.

They took the electricity supply for the light station from the mains in our tram terminus, and as we assisted the electricians we quickly got to know Mr March. He had been a Trinity House lighthouse keeper, working the lights of the Western Approaches to the English Channel, Lundy, Fastnet and latterly the Needles, which he liked the best because he had been allowed to live on the Isle of Wight. Now, he explained, on the point of retirement, he had been seconded to the Admiralty to be put in charge of the new pier light, not so much a beacon like the others as one whose purpose was to send coded messages to shipping and especially to submarines. He proudly pointed to the RN on his cap and the anchors on his lapels, evidence of his new position.

He seemed to find our company agreeable and possibly a relief from the tedium of his job: most of his days were spent watching the English Channel through naval glasses with headphones on to receive his Admiralty orders. We started taking our meals together and before long he found that he preferred the tram's stew-pot to his own staple of boiled beef and biscuits. Thus in the evenings he would explain to us the details of Royal Navy light code, based as it was at this time on Morse, and changed for security reasons each month. We also learned the significance of King's Regulations, the manual of which, with all the references to the keeping of on-shore lights carefully underlined, was always carried on his person. Strangely, Duncan also took to King's Regulations and would pore over them by the hour, sitting beside Eddie in his tiny operations room whenever we were not running the tram. Under Eddie's tuition he learned how to use both receiver and transmitter.

It was a curious fact, and one which I had noticed before, that when anyone was disposed to help Duncan the fact that he couldn't speak seemed to be a matter of no consequence at all.

Chapter Twelve

IT WAS WELL FOR US that we had found such an important new companion, for we were in the process of losing several older ones. Both battalions of the West Sussex Fusiliers had been sent to France, Rifleman Kelly with them, and in February Mr Parker, our great benefactor, closed his store in Worthing and moved to Reigate, although he made arrangements which allowed our tram to continue operating, which was after Sayers had gone. However, one person stayed put. That was Mr Schwayder, and he was busy converting Goring Hall into a military hospital or what was now called a Casualty Clearing Station. In doing this he had the help of Hattie and ourselves, Hattie in charge of dismantling the chandeliers, mirrors and the gilded panelling, and us to carry them to the basement to be kept there for the duration of the war.

This meant that after an interval of several weeks we had for the weekdays come back to live in the old tram. Our return had the most extraordinary effect on Homer, who galloped around his paddock whinnying repeatedly, as though he could scent a mare. This strange behaviour continued for two days, then on the third he lay on the ground exhausted by his efforts, or so we thought. But on the fourth day we found him dead.

We were dumbfounded at such a tragedy. Homer had been so central in our lives. He had taken us from London to Canterbury, with all that had happened there, including the battle when he certainly saved us from being overrun. After that affair it was Homer who decided where we should go next, when he turned away from Canterbury and Margate and took us southwards to the sea and finally to Sussex and the haven of Mr Schwayder's paddock.

Homer couldn't just be taken away by kennel-men, and we decided that he must be suitably committed to the earth. Therefore Hattie prevailed upon Mr Schwayder to arrange for his gardeners to dig a grave in the field beside the sea, into which, when it was completed, Homer's body was dragged, and she even got a clergyman to say his piece at the burial. At the last minute we remembered the signboard with Canterbury on it, and this we buried beside Homer, in gypsy fashion, since Hattie, like all gypsies, believes in providing essentials for the afterlife.

At the conclusion of this sad event I turned back and saw that watching these proceedings from the top step of the tram was Tiger, motionless, with his head ever so slightly lowered and bearing the most solemn expression that I ever witnessed.

We decided to spend the rest of the day and the following night where we were. We were disturbed by the day's events, and in any case the winter night was densely foggy. We cooked a meal and tried to relax listening to the wireless, but when we turned in we remained wakeful. At midnight we put on the news and at the end the announcer came back with an item just in: a bomb had been dropped on the pier at Brighton. The awful feeling came over us that it could so easily have been Worthing and not Brighton, and this did nothing to help us sleep.

So uneasy did Duncan and I feel that we got up as soon as dawn began to show, and still in dense fog, the three of us got on our bicycles and went to the old pier.

We passed Hattie's house and dropped her off there, but as we neared the sea-front Tiger's hackles seemed to rise and rise, probably because he missed Homer, we said. Here the fog became so dense that we didn't see the pier until we were right on it, which made it all the more awful when we did. What we found was a scene of terrible devastation, for a bomb had hit the ballroom.

A few firemen and a civil defence squad were still standing at the head of what had been the pier, though it was obvious that there was not much for them to do and no one for them to rescue. They said the bomb was a thousand-pounder and had landed smack on the ballroom just after eight o'clock; they let us on to the pier to look for our belongings.

Our tram was still there – just. It had been lifted off its rails and rested at an absurd angle on the timbers of the pier, its windows blown out by the blast. Beyond the tram the ballroom had gone altogether and we picked our way across its wreckage to the light station to find out for ourselves what, if any of it, remained. It was obvious that there was no chance that Mr March could have survived, and although the rescue workers had searched for him they had found nothing. They said they would search again for his body as soon as the light improved.

'Brighton pier gone as well?' I asked one of the firemen.

'No,' he said, 'that was just a mistake.'

The days went by and the civil defence workers departed, leaving the wreckage and our broken tram to us, the tram standing like a sentinel defying the destruction around it and now directly overlooking the sea.

We went again to search the light station's remains. Mr March's body had not been recovered, but we found his overcoat and jacket still hanging on a wall that was left standing and in the jacket we found his code book, and also – which was good news for Duncan – his copies of King's Regulations and Admiralty Instructions. Amazingly, the light itself had survived the bombing, partly because it was facing seawards; also the hoist was still there. These important pieces of equipment must, we decided, be saved before the whole structure collapsed into the sea.

We retraced our steps and carried out a careful inspection of the tram. Its iron framework was intact and we could see that the damage was mainly to the windows and to the interior, which had been thoroughly blasted – so thoroughly that there would have been no chance of our surviving had we been there, as we would have been if Homer hadn't died. The engine, which was beneath the floor at the rear, was unharmed and so to our amazement was the electricity at the terminus, which evidently no one had thought to disconnect. The force of the blast had lifted the tram into the air and it had landed to one side, breaking the bogies and two of the wheels, resulting in the angle at which it was now pitched. The pier beneath, with its surface of railway sleepers, was intact, as were the supporting steel piles driven into the seabed. We realised that we might after all be able to rescue it – at least as a stationary tram.

We returned to Hattie's and told her what we had found. There was silence as the news sank in. After a minute she said, and it was her only comment, 'Then it is the end. Homer knew.'

'But don't you see, Hattie, it's not the end, it is not the end,' we said in chorus, me with words and Duncan with his signs. 'We have still got us, us and our tram.'

'But what use is a bombed tram?'

'I don't know,' I said. 'I don't know. We shall just have to wait and see what we can do.'

The next day we collected the gear we needed from Mr Schwayder's, with the promise from one of the gardeners of assistance if any was needed and then we started salvaging from the end of the pier. We dismantled the naval light and the iron platform on which it was mounted, and in doing so we were careful to examine its layout and see exactly how it operated. We found the Admiralty radio receiver and transmitter, and retrieved from the sea when the tide went out a locker full of spares and accessories, including a convex mirror two feet across (such as a conventional lighthouse has), also the naval glasses. Then we dismantled the hoist and carried everything piece by piece across the twisted girders where the ballroom had been and piled it all up beside the tram. The extent of what we were able to retrieve surprised us, and it was a full week's labour.

After this we started work on the tram itself, first raising it with jacks on to blocks to make it stable. We reduced the tilt to something that made it possible to move about inside, though the front section never quite lost its rakish appearance. We then repaired the exterior, filling the holes in the damaged plates and replacing the glass of the windows, for which we now had to use ordinary window glass. It was quite unsuitable, but was all that was available, and we figured that for a tram which was not going to run any more this would scarcely matter.

In this way, painstakingly during the next few weeks, we rebuilt our tram until it was quite reborn and, painted in the same dark green as the light station had been painted, it looked fit for the new role that we intended for it.

For by now we had formed a plan. We would reconstruct the signalling light on the top of the tram and make a tiny operations room, large enough for one person, and if the Admiralty had lost the services of Mr March we, or to be exact

Duncan, would operate the light in his place. Furthermore, when the supply boat arrived – for this was the rather curious method the Admiralty used for provisioning – we would have the hoist in place to raise the boxes, just as Mr March had done. When it came to operating the light station I must admit that I had little idea of how much Duncan had learned from Eddie March, but when he started to receive and transmit, the extent of his expertise was clear. He was determined that the light should resume its part in the South Coast signalling system. There was though the small matter of the call code which changed by the month, and how we were to obtain the next one, which was nearly due, was far from clear.

At this stage Hattie rejoined us and, watching our efforts, began to recover her own confidence in the tram. She set about making a galley for cooking and new blackout curtains. Then, unknown to me, she made a uniform for Duncan which was indistinguishable from that which Mr March had worn, complete with its naval insignia and a cap on which were the letters RN. Of course, this was not her idea but Duncan's, though by this time Hattie was so besotted by him that she would probably have dressed him up in anything he asked for.

When I saw Duncan in all this gear I must confess that I lost my temper. 'You are mad,' I shouted. 'Can't you see, it's a lie and you're an impostor. Why pretend to be a naval officer when you are Duncan and don't need to be anyone else? Besides, they could put you in jail if they found you wearing all this stuff.'

I fully expected that Duncan would see the sense of this and throw his 'naval' cap into the sea, but unfortunately this did not happen. Instead he just stood there looking angry and then turned and walked away. The trouble was that Hattie obviously agreed with him, and I was left feeling guilty and had plenty of time to wonder what hot water we were going to get into next.

Chapter Thirteen

FOR THE SEQUEL WE DID not have long to wait, for one morning a naval launch appeared and tied up alongside the hoist below the tram. I shouted to Duncan, who pretended not to hear me and remained hunched up in his operations room with his naval cap, intently watching the horizon through Mr March's naval glasses.

Two officers from the Admiralty climbed our steps, and naturally they asked for Mr March. I led them on to the new promontory we had constructed in front of the tram, and waved my arm in the direction of Duncan.

'Up there,' I said. 'Change of quarters after the bomb, but everything still working. I am afraid he can't hear you.' It suddenly dawned on me that Duncan dressed up in Hattie's uniform was the split image of Eddie March.

'He's OK, then? We heard he might have copped it.'

'He's fine,' I lied. 'Probably used to these sort of ups and downs.'

'Then we won't disturb him, just give him his new codes and then we'll fetch his supplies and be off.' We shook hands.

I felt even more fraudulent when, as they departed, they turned and gave Duncan a naval salute.

A much sterner test took place some weeks later at the sinking of the SS *Carinthia*, the most dramatic event on the home front until this time and one which had far-ranging effects on how people viewed the war. Hitherto this war had happened only on the Continent or somewhere else, but this disaster brought it dramatically close to home.

The *Carinthia* was a Cunard White Star liner sailing from New York and bound for Harwich. She was torpedoed at night by a German submarine, and sank about seven miles from the coast off Worthing. A rescue attempt was mounted and lifeboats from all the local stations were called out, including those from Bognor, Littlehampton, Brighton and, of course, our own. The West Worthing lifeboat launched right behind us, beside the Aircraft Listening Station with the sound detectors and the air-raid siren, and as it entered the water the coxswain steered so that he came right beneath us on the tram.

'For Chrissake give us a light to lay a course by,' he shouted.

'OK,' I yelled back, and the boat disappeared into the murk.

The problem, as we quickly saw, was that Duncan's signalling light had a limited range and it could only help them for their first two miles, so we set it to go off at fixed ten-second interval, which was its best effect. Then we got the big reflector, which was capable of sending its beam to the far horizon, and bolted its turntable so that the reflector could rotate about the light.

The difficulty was that the only means of rotating it was by its emergency turning handle which took both hands to operate. This was heavy work and we had to take it in turns, though with the help of some grease we managed to get it to go round quite evenly. We set it on an arc of sixty degrees and switched the light to continuous, after which there was nothing for it but to go on turning throughout the night.

At dawn our lifeboat returned to refuel and immediately went out again. But as they were leaving they sailed in close and the whole crew gave us a thumbs-up sign as we lit them on their way. By the time full light came, we were collapsed with fatigue.

Two days later the newspapers had the full story: of the *Carinthia*'s seven hundred passengers and crew, all but forty-five were rescued and carried to safety. Our lifeboat had been first on the scene and with the other lifeboats had picked up those in the water, then ferried to and fro between the *Carinthia* and a naval frigate which had come on the scene. Fortunately, the *Carinthia* had sunk slowly, for it had been unable to launch its own lifeboats. The West Worthing coxswain received a commendation and one of the national newspapers even referred to the 'West Worthing naval beacon', which was what they called it, 'set up on an old tram on the remains of the pier'. Later a photographer from the local newspaper arrived and took pictures which showed Duncan in his operating room and the tram on its promontory resting at a jaunty angle.

Then *The Times* did an article on the resourcefulness of the British in time of war in which the episode was mentioned. They even gave the name Duncan Scrutton, although we never discovered how they got it.

One evening two weeks later a letter addressed to Duncan Scrutton Esq. arrived by special messenger, who insisted that his instructions were to deliver it personally to Mr Scrutton. I had to call Duncan down. Then we saw the word 'Admiralty' in embossed letters on the back of the envelope, and both of us had the same prickling on the back of our necks. Duncan, who was quite fired up, handed it to me to open.

I read out: 'Sir, Your efforts add a new chapter to the brave history of our ancient Southern ports in their defeat of our enemies. Let the German Navy beware. Signed Winston S. Churchill, Lord Warden of the Cinque Ports and First Lord of—'

That was as far as I got. A wild beast's roar

came from Duncan and he rushed towards me. 'Stinker Potts, *Stinker Potts*,' he screamed. It was the first time he had ever repeated anything.

'No,' I cried. 'Don't you see it's not, it's Winnie.'

He seized the letter from my hands and in fury tore it into pieces. What followed made the affair of the popadoms seem like a summer's afternoon. He stormed about the tram, seizing anything he could lay his hands on and hurling it on the floor. Hattie dived under one of the benches and stayed there. I pleaded, everything I could think of, but the anger just poured out of him. It was as though a surgeon had stuck his knife into an abscess and the pent-up pus came bursting forth. I could never have imagined that the name Stinker Potts, or what he took for it, could have evoked such a fearful response, or indeed what must have been so much pain.

The only person to be unaffected by all this was Tiger, who slept on his front seat unconcerned by what was going on around him, and when, anxious for him, I went and sat beside him he looked up at me disdainfully.

Finally, when the tumult ended he got up, stretched himself, and settled down in a new position.

Eventually it was sleep that overcame Duncan also.

Chapter Fourteen

SOMEHOW WE SURVIVED this volcanic erup-
tion, and Mr Churchill's letter and its destruction were never mentioned again. Mr Churchill
himself was now continuously in the news as he
had just become Prime Minister in place of Mr
Chamberlain. By this time the Germans had
nearly beaten the French, and one of Mr
Churchill's first acts was to bring the British
Army home from France, or rather from Dunkirk, where it mainly was at the time. Quite why
it was there in the first place was something we
could never understand, unless it was a mistake,
but clearly to get it home was going to be a
difficult job with the Germans everywhere.

Mr Churchill decided to send the Navy to
Dunkirk to get it, but a lot of smaller boats were
needed to ferry the men from the shore to the

big ships standing further out, and the call went out to all the boatmen and lifeboats of the south coast to assemble at Dunkirk. They responded even from as far afield as the Isle of Wight, which sent its two paddle steamers. At the same time the light stations sprang into life all along the coast, and from our position we could see the Hove light on one side and the Littlehampton one on the other. Our light was ordered to be one of the chain, and after our experience with the *Carinthia* we knew we must get the automatic turntable into operation.

We found a number of its pieces in the locker and reassembled them, and Duncan spent a day and a half making the missing bits. Then we went to the Aircraft Listening Station and managed to borrow an electric motor, which had its own generator. By the time the armada of small boats was properly under way, our light was operational and we could provide the fixed point they needed for their navigation. This was vital, because between us and Angmering there were a number of shallow sandbanks where inshore ships had come to grief in the past, especially at the Church Rocks off Kingston Gorse, known to us because we once used to catch lobsters there.

After the first four days, when all the boats were going eastwards, the pattern of sailing altered, for after reaching the French coast they could only work for as long as they had fuel in their tanks, after which they had to return to Dover or Folkestone to refuel. But, as we heard later, the delays at these ports were soon so long that they scarcely had enough fuel to stay in the queue. Therefore they mostly opted to refuel at their home ports and began sailing across us, first one way and then the other. They also brought back soldiers whom they landed at any of the piers or harbours they passed along the way. In the case of the Worthing lifeboat and any others that accompanied it, the delivery point was ourselves, and we therefore contrived a small jetty where we had erected the hoist. At this time we were working the light night and day, with two of us keeping the watch while the other slept, and this continued for almost three weeks from May into June. In the later stages there was a procession of shattered men, most of whom were wounded. So many of them were landed on our pier that we wondered if the word had got round that Hattie had arranged for all casualties to be taken to Goring Hall and had even organised for Mr Schwayder's car to collect them. On one occasion there were so many that Goring Hall became full, even to the corridors, and Hattie had to take her load to the next casualty clearing station along the coast.

She told us afterwards about this experience. The CCS was an old house called, she thought, Greenways. The man in charge, who wore army uniform, was tall, with a moustache, and extremely brusque. But then, she told us happily, he relented and by the time she left he was pressing her to return with another load of casualties. She added, 'Funny, he was called Scrutton, too, Captain Robert Scrutton.'

'Seems you made quite a conquest there,' I said.

'Oh I don't think so,' said Hattie coyly.

'You'll see,' snapped Duncan, adding another sign which it was as well Hattie didn't see.

It was a great surprise when one of the last of the casualties proved to be none other than our old friend Rifleman Kelly, or rather Sergeant-Major Kelly, for his rank had been restored to him. His leg was heavily splinted and bandaged, and we had to use the hoist to lift him from the boat.

' 'Fraid I caught a packet, but 'ad to make it back to the old tram somehow if I was going to die,' he said carelessly.

We hurriedly got him taken to hospital, with Hattie accompanying him, and I think it was she who prevailed on Mr Schwayder to get a special surgeon from East Grinstead Hospital, who operated on him. This was carried out at Mr Schwayder's own expense, and to our great relief Sergeant Kelly survived.

The incident drew the three of us back to Goring Hall which, in the aftermath of Dunkirk, had been upgraded to a field hospital and greatly enlarged by the building of Nissen huts to provide wards. Apart from those provided by the Army, its staff were all local volunteers, and when the evacuation from France ended and we had returned to the earlier role of naval signalling, we went there more and more to help. Hattie became a VAD and took to nursing in eight-hour shifts while Duncan and I took it in turns to act as ward orderlies when we were not on our own duty on the tram.

This was a respite of sorts, but it was not to last long. We were reminded almost daily that the

Germans were on the other side of the Channel as more and more aircraft began to fill our skies. Then, at the beginning of August, waves of bombers came to bomb London and the Battle of Britain started. We had a grandstand view of the dog-fights, but it also meant that the lifeboat was in constant operation to retrieve pilots from the sea and often they were landed on our pier. Once we picked up a German aircrew, who filed ashore in their strange grey uniforms and each, as he passed beneath Duncan's observation post, stopped, clicked heels and saluted; quite rightly, I thought, since he had played a part in the saving of their lives, as no doubt they were aware.

After this we lived in the tram all the time and each evening listened to the wireless, which gave the number of German planes shot down that day, first fifty or sixty, and finally the dizzy total of a hundred and eighty-six one day in late August.

This provoked a wave of national rejoicing, and it certainly had an electrifying effect upon Duncan, who was glued to the wireless day and night. When the air battles were overhead he would lie on the top of the tram, training his naval glasses on the planes above and quite oblivious of his own danger. I was more cautious and usually climbed below the decking of the pier.

Chapter Fifteen

IN SEPTEMBER THE GERMANS changed their tactics and began to bomb our airfields. We saw many more of their fighters, which cleared a pathway for the Stukas, the dive-bombers that followed. Once we watched an attack on Tangmere aerodrome at Arundel, some ten miles away, by a string of bombers which, as they reached a certain point, suddenly dived vertically in turn, the thud of the bombs coming a few seconds later. They seemed to have it all their own way.

Then from the roof of the tram we saw three Stukas coming in over the sea towards us and realised it was going to be our turn next, their target obviously the Aircraft Listening Station on the shore behind us. We knew from Eddie March that it was much more than just a listening post: it was part of a secret early-warning system, and evidently the Germans knew this, too.

Yelling for Duncan to follow, I leapt down the ladder to the top deck and then down the stairway and under the tram just as the first Stuka dived, its siren blaring.

The bomb missed the post and landed in the field behind with a shattering explosion that shook the tram and what was left of the pier. I yelled again for Duncan, who still hadn't come.

The second Stuka came shrieking down and this time the bomb nearly hit us, landing in the sea and sending a shower of debris all over us. It was quickly followed by the third, which mercifully was the last, but either it failed to release its bomb or else the bomb didn't explode. The screaming siren was all that I heard.

Frantic with anxiety I climbed out and rushed to the top of the tram. Duncan lay face upwards covered in seaweed and sand, and my heart was in my mouth for I thought he must be dead. Then I saw that in his hand he held a catapult at the ready, and I knew that he was alive. He sat up, grinning, and wiped away some of the debris and I could see that there was a pile of small stones beside where he had lain.

'Got 'im!' he shouted. It was just the fifth word he had ever uttered.

'Don't be daft, Duncan.' I was shouting myself on account of my anxiety. 'Of course you didn't. He just didn't pull out of his dive.' But Duncan waved his catapult triumphantly and pointed.

Then I saw a most marvellous sight. The Stuka had failed to pull out of its dive and had embedded itself in the water and the soft sand beneath, from which its tail alone stuck upwards lapped gently by the waves, like some monstrous javelin that had been hurled from the sky.

The extraordinary spectacle soon drew spectators from far and wide, who lined the sea-front to stare at the grey tailplane with its red and black swastika. At the same time as they were gazing at it, the crew of the early warning station were hard at work dismantling their equipment and piling it into the heavy vehicles that held the great dishes that distinguished them. By the evening they had moved off to a new position, security, or at least discretion, evidently being uppermost in their minds.

In their place the press arrived and, since the tram was closest to the wrecked plane, that is where they came to take their pictures.

At this point the situation took an altogether new turn, which brought about the most extraordinary change in our circumstances imaginable. With the departure of the Early Warning Station, both the onlookers and the press concluded – and nothing seemed to deflect them from this view – that our tram was the principal object of the attack. The imaginative ones assumed it to be a disguise which concealed, perhaps, some secret weapon within, and even Duncan's defending the tram with only his catapult was believed to be part of the ingenious subterfuge – it was only the Admiralty uniform he wore which gave the game away.

Therefore the photographers focused their efforts on ourselves, and particularly on Duncan, who posed, catapult in hand, with the tailplane of the Stuka forming the background. They could scarcely take enough pictures. It led to Duncan returning to the roof of the tram once more, where, with the help of the remaining stones, he demonstrated his prowess by letting fly at the remnants of the Stuka some forty or fifty yards away for their benefit. Such was his accuracy that its fabric began to dent and eventually a hole appeared. The reporters were agog.

In the same way as they had been quite happy from the start to invent their story from the evidence in front of them, now they quickly decided that Duncan really had shot down the Stuka, and unfortunately Duncan by his gestures did nothing to discourage this interpretation. The small matter of his not being able to reply to their questions seemed to them in their eagerness in no way extraordinary. They simply decided that Duncan was one of the strong, silent sort, or else happened to suffer from an excess of natural modesty.

When the reporters were unable to get answers from Duncan, they began to turn their attention to me, but the excuses I started to offer for Duncan's supposed success failed to satisfy them and were not all well received.

This was brought home to me by an American reporter, who cut me short when I was trying to explain.

'Let me tell ya, young fella, that what we care

about in Texas is an action man like Mr Scrutton. We don't give as much as a piss for words, and as for explanations we leave those to the likes of Abe Lincoln.' He must have seen that I looked crestfallen for he added, 'And y'know, Bud, something I'll tell ya, this is the best story we gotten into since the animals went in two by two.'

After this I saw that it was better for me to keep my mouth shut and allow the press and Duncan to sort out the matter between them. In no time at all he was decided to be the hero of the hour.

Thereafter, what these gentlemen reported, their editors elaborated in turn, with the result that the national newspapers all carried different accounts of the new hero, Mr Scrutton the lightkeeper on the tram, who had managed to shoot down a German aircraft with only a catapult. The subject soon became a matter of competition between one newspaper and another.

'152 planes, one shot down by catapult', ran the banner headline of the *Daily Mail*.

'David slays Goliath all over again', boomed *The Times*, and there started to appear in the letters page explanations by learned professors of why a successful shot by a catapult was likely – or unlikely.

The nation's morale was definitely boosted, and the stories and letters continued for some time, but the third day after the event the tailplane itself retired gracefully, sliding into the water and disintegrating. Not long afterwards its bomb, a three-hundred-pounder, was washed from the wreck and on to the beach, at which point we were evacuated while it was being made safe and carted away.

For me the disappearance of the reporters and onlookers came as a relief, though for Duncan it was a source of great disappointment. To make matters worse, we now received from the Admiralty a signal that all lights were stood down, 'except for emergencies, when you will be notified at the time'.

Chapter Sixteen

CELEBRITY, THEY SAY, always comes at a price, and I dare say that this is true even when the celebrity is as short-lived as ours was. The price, so far as we were concerned, was that we came, for the first time perhaps, to the notice of Authority.

An envelope arrived addressed to Duncan Scrutton Esq. and this time it had no Admiralty mark on it or anything else. It was a simple brown paper affair and the letter inside informed us that he would shortly be called upon, like others of his age group, for National Service. It said that there would be an interval of three months before his actual call-up, and that in due course he would be given a time and place at which to report for a medical examination to confirm or otherwise his fitness to serve.

It had never occurred to any of us that this might happen, although it should have been entirely forseeable, since we knew plenty of people who had been called up and Duncan was now nearly twenty. My first thought was that we should go on the run and this time that was Hattie's opinion, too. But to my surprise Duncan's response was entirely different: he was full of enthusiasm and bursting with patriotism. We had long talks about which service he should choose and in the end he decided upon the army, rather than the navy, on the grounds that although he had a suitable uniform he didn't think he could face the seasickness. The fact that he couldn't speak, and that this would make his selection for any branch of service unlikely, was not mentioned.

A short time later the letter arrived instructing Duncan to appear for medical examination by a Dr J. Fortescue, No. 16, The Saltings, Worthing. We could hardly complain that this was inconvenient, although it seemed an odd address for such an examination, since it was just off our own Grand Avenue.

After giving the matter some thought we decided that I should accompany Duncan, in case I was needed to give answers to any questions the doctor might ask him.

On the day we walked the short distance to The Saltings, a terrace of white stucco houses, and climbed the steps of No. 16. It bore a plate on which was the doctor's name, although we were somewhat confused because this had Dr ffortescue with two small fs. We were shown into a waiting room with heavy velvet curtains, a large mahogany sideboard and a dining table which bore old copies of *Picture Post* and *Weekly Illustrated*. Others of our own age sat on chairs around. Duncan was given a form on which to enter illnesses from which he had suffered, and put down measles and chicken pox.

'What about meningitis?' I suggested, but Duncan shook his head.

When his turn came we went together to the first floor where an army corporal asked which of us was D. Scrutton. When this was determined I was dispatched to wait downstairs but at that moment Dr Fortescue appeared and with a wave of his arm I was allowed to remain.

He was certainly quite unlike any doctor that we had come across and, what with his address in central Worthing, he didn't seem to be at all the sort of doctor you would expect to be carrying out call-up medicals. He was tall, with brushed-back grey hair, very elegant and carefully groomed. He wore a smartly tailored black coat with tails, and grey striped trousers; also he had on spats and wore a monocle.

His manner was oddly bright. 'What's an old-timer like you doing joining the Colours?' he asked as he began to read Duncan's history sheet. 'Never mind, that's a thing I have to admire. I am sure we can get through this quite quickly.'

Duncan had to undress and this was something that made me wonder, for I realised that until then I had never seen my brother in his birthday suit. He did indeed look quite old and he also seemed shorter, or perhaps we had grown and he hadn't.

The examination proceeded, and the only hitch was when the doctor advanced upon Duncan holding a large rubber hammer, at which Duncan let out a nervous 'Watsit'.

'Just a patella hammer, nothing to it at all,' said Dr Fortescue, proceeding to tap him in various places.

After that came the eye test which was the one we had been nervous about, since Duncan wouldn't have been able to say the letters. However Dr Fortescue just asked him if he could read the bottom line and when Duncan nodded he appeared to be satisfied. And that seemed to be that: Duncan was passed fit for Military Service, in spite of his not being able to speak.

'Go and serve your country, my brave man,' said Dr Fortescue, screwing in his monocle, which made him look even more maniacal, and he shook Duncan by the hand. 'One day come back and tell me all about it.' He beamed, then added, 'If you come back, that is.'

It is the case that if there was a strange character in Worthing we never failed to find him, or perhaps it was just the effect that the sea air had on people. For Duncan it was all too good to be true, although later I was to ask myself how it was that I, too, was swept along by all this. The fact is that Duncan carried such conviction that we neither of us questioned it; also he had this uncanny ability to turn situations to his advantage or what he considered that to be.

I prayed that this might last.

Chapter Seventeen

WE WERE NOW STAYING at Hattie's and going each day to the wreck of our tram to see if any cables had arrived from the Admiralty. It is sad to have to say that, much to Duncan's chagrin, no further instructions arrived. However, what there was to collect was a daily postbag of letters addressed to Duncan Scrutton or sometimes just Duncan. These came for the most part from admiring ladies, being written in highly expressive terms and sometimes accompanied by photographs of the writer, occasionally quite explicit. These last were particular favourites and Duncan papered the walls of his bedroom with them, much to Hattie's irritation when she returned from the shifts she was working at Goring Hall.

Then into this cosy domestic scene there

arrived a letter of a very different sort: printed unmistakably on the back of the envelope were the words 'Buckingham Palace'. It stated that His Majesty had been pleased to bestow on Mr Duncan Scrutton the honour of becoming a Member of the Order of the British Empire. If he would kindly let the writer know whether this honour was acceptable, he would be told the date of an early investiture to be held at Buckingham Palace.

Duncan received this news somewhat coldly; he said he wouldn't mind accepting the honour but in no circumstances would he be able to leave his signalling station – since at any moment it might require his attention, and certainly he could not take the risk of going to London. Anyway, he added, he believed that he was a member of the British Empire already.

This was a great disappointment to me, and I did all I could to persuade Duncan to change his mind and collect the decoration, which he had surely earned, but to no effect, so I wrote a letter explaining matters as politely as I could.

Time passed and we forgot about it. We began the repair of the tram afresh and gradually it started to assume its old appearance – or better, since the last of the bomb explosions had blown it upright again. After this Duncan restored his light signal in the hope that he might receive a new instruction.

Then one day a van drew up and five policemen got out. This was somewhat alarming and made me start to wonder what trouble it was that we had got into now, though Duncan believed it just meant that his call-up had arrived. But the policemen remained standing there in a row, and then a very large car drew up. Its doors were opened and to our astonishment out stepped the King and then the Queen, followed by a number of men all in smart suits wearing bowler hats and carrying furled umbrellas. One of them came to explain that His Majesty had understood Mr Scrutton's reluctance to leave his station and had chosen instead to bestow his honour on Mr Scrutton here. The King had also expressed the wish to see the tram from which the German bomber had been shot down.

So we were all presented and the King and Queen mounted our steps and came aboard the tram. The King was in the smart uniform of one of the Guards regiments and wore a most becoming black cap which had a lot of gold braid. He may have been surprised to find that Duncan also was wearing uniform, but if so he was too polite to mention it.

It was rather stiff, and not much was said until the Queen saw Tiger and asked his name and, when I told her, she said that they had a Tiger, too. This helped to break the ice and also drew the King into conversation. It was apparent that he had a most terrible stutter, although this did not prevent him from asking me all sorts of questions about what we had done and how the signal station had worked during the time of Dunkirk.

Then he wanted Duncan to show him exactly where the German plane had come down, and how he had shot it with his catapult. Duncan pointed to the ladder leading to the roof of the tram and the next moment, to everyone's surprise, the two of them climbed up the ladder and disappeared from view. The gentlemen in suits attempted to follow, but the King signalled them to return to the lower deck, where the Queen was soon in deep conversation with Hattie. Some five minutes passed and then I began to worry lest the King had fallen over the side, or something terrible, and furtively climbed to the roof to satisfy myself.

What I beheld was very extraordinary. The King, who I was relieved to see was securely clutching the tram's conductor-arm, and Duncan were having a conversation in Duncan's sign language. Or to be more exact, Duncan was instructing the King like a teacher, with the King as his pupil copying Duncan's signs as he tried to learn them. The King was clearly engrossed and was following intently every move that Duncan made. And for good measure whenever the King got a sign right Duncan would take his catapult and loose off a stone at one of the breakwaters, using them for targets. I stood there and watched for several moments, but then the King caught sight of me standing at the top of the ladder and his manner changed and the magic evaporated. Soon he gathered himself together and climbed down to rejoin the Queen.

A short ceremony followed at which Duncan received his decoration and here a serious hitch in proceedings almost happened which I was only just able to avert. The attendants stood in a circle and the one beside the King held a tray on

which were decorations of various kinds. Out of
the corner of my eye I saw Duncan begin to raise
his arm and I realised that he was looking
intently at a decoration which bore the label
'Star of India'. I realised that he was quite
capable of asking the King to give it to him
and – who knows? – in the King's immediate
state of mind, he might have done so.

On such occasions I always keep the toe of
my boot on the tender part of Duncan's heel and
now as I put on the pressure his arm came down,
and to my great relief the King picked up the
intended MBE and hung its ribbon round Duncan's neck.

At the close of the ceremony the King made
an impromptu speech, which, considering his
stutter, was brave of him. It ended with the
words: 'Our splendid people, our marvellous
island, this pearl w . . . w . . .'

'Washed,' said Duncan.

'Washed, thank you, w . . . washed by the
silver sea.'

At these fine words the gentlemen of the
travelling court beamed with delight, and a small
one at the back started clapping his hands. The
Queen also smiled, but she had been smiling all

along, and now she stepped forward and took the King gently by the arm.

Then I distinctly heard her say, 'Come along, Bertie.'

Chapter Eighteen

WHAT WE HAD NOT realised was that the press
was busily engaged in covering the King's visit,
although on account of security their cameras
and reporters were kept out of sight, along with
the general public. Therefore the next day all the
papers carried pictures of the King with Duncan
on the tram's roof and in them it was the body
language that said everything. It was exactly the
story the editors needed, since there wasn't
much to say about the war, which at that time
was either going badly or stuck in a dull patch.
The ceremony of Duncan's MBE brightened
things up and began a new wave of acclaim
which the feature-writers fuelled by retelling the
story of our tram from the time it took over as
signalling station before Dunkirk.

Early each morning Duncan would leave

Hattie's house with Tiger, claiming that he was looking for the cable he still expected to arrive from the Admiralty, but in reality in order to collect his daily postbag of fan mail. He remained in the tram for most of the day while he opened and read the letters, and if the weather was bad as it usually was that December Duncan persuaded himself that he should sleep there as well, since he believed that at any time he might be called upon for a submarine in distress or an air crew downed in the sea.

The fact that he was spending the nights there was a matter of concern to Hattie and myself, for I felt that to some extent this was a sort of private camouflage and concealed a deeper malaise.

It was our worry that all the attention was beginning to go to Duncan's head, because sometimes his behaviour was now not altogether in character. Yet if I mentioned anything he would reply coldly that his time was short because at any moment he might be called up. But it was a haunted Duncan: we felt that there were things going on in his head, troubles which he would not disclose. He moved about much more slowly, pondering, as if on some mission of his own. I even thought that perhaps his appearance was changing, too, for he looked older again and somehow contracted. It was all a very great mystery.

In January, though, we had a small break-through. We managed to get Duncan away from the tram for a few hours to watch Charlie Chaplin in *The Great Dictator* which was on at the Odeon in Worthing. We laughed at Charlie's version of the preposterous Hitler and found again for a short while the spirit that we had had when we first went to Mr Schwayder's.

The sun came out but then went behind a cloud again, and the respite proved to be all too brief. Indeed, what followed was far worse than just a cloud, for on 21 January, although the dawn broke clear and off to the tram went Duncan and Tiger, as the day went on the wind rose ominously and by early afternoon it was blowing a gale. By evening the gale had become a hurricane in which it was impossible even to stand outside. I put on the Home Service, loudly to keep my spirits up, and listened to its weather reports through the evening. I knew that I should be alone that night, for neither Hattie at Mr Schwayder's nor Duncan at the tram had any chance of returning in such conditions. I remained awake.

At about three o'clock in the morning I put on my foul-weather things, took a torch and went outside. The rain swept down but it was just possible to move by holding on to something for support. Along the front a huge sea was running, which made me wonder what it was like if you were a sailor, or even on a pier. I clutched the railing that bordered the pavement of the sea-front, and certainly I was the only living thing that moved there.

But then I could not find the pier. I turned about and felt the full force of the rain as it whipped my face and soon, even though I wore a sou'wester, I was wet. I retraced my steps and walked the whole length of the pavement for a second time, the waves crashing against the low cliff beneath. I was increasingly terrified. Then lightning burst over the sea and I saw in that instant that there was no pier, there was no tram. There was only the fearsome, pounding sea.

I froze in disbelief as the awful reality penetrated my brain that Duncan and Tiger must have been swept away.

Frantically I ran this way and that and in the

end I just stood there, paralysed, beside that roaring, white in the lightning, surge. I could see now that the shoreline was pure and uninterrupted on either side as far as the eye could make it out, just the cliffs and the sea as it had been through all creation, the burden of man cast off. My torch went out. The devastation without was nothing compared with the devastation inside my head.

I could not think what I was to do.

I fell on my knees and prayed, devastated by an awful lack of purpose, and all that time the storm streamed over me. Had not some police come along I would have remained there till dawn.

It was the next day before the full impact of the tragedy hit me and by then Hattie had returned and we could share our bereavement. The police came and we went with them to the pier, or to where we thought the pier had been, for even in the clear light of day you could not tell exactly where, for the tide was high and as the waves broke not a trace of it was to be seen.

The tram was there. Its shattered hulk was upright, on top of the cliff where the sea had deposited it, a bare skeleton of the tram it once had been. It stuck up to the sky like some monument of war. It was surely the mute obelisk of all the endeavours of us three.

Two days later, still numbed by grief, Hattie and I sat in the front room of her house and were gazing in silence out of the window. Outside was a scene of contrasting peace, for the sun was shining, when all of a sudden it seemed that we were witnessing an apparition, which for an instant made us think that time had taken leave of its senses and was going backwards. It wasn't though, it was quite real. Walking unhurriedly up the garden path there came, as if back from the dead, a dishevelled but undaunted Tiger.

I can tell you we cried and cried.

Chapter Nineteen

IT DID NOT TAKE US long to realise that in his final days Duncan had known something we did not know, and by his dying in such a way he bequeathed to us a mystery – which it remains, and we dwell upon it still.

As the news got round, we received many messages of support. An inquest was held which concluded that Duncan, whose body had not been found, was missing, presumed drowned. Everything that followed was arranged by Mr Schwayder. One February morning about three weeks later, a service in Duncan's memory was held, not in church but on the cliff overlooking the sea beside the wreck of the tram.

The sun shone with all the conviction of spring, and the service was conducted by the Bishop of Chichester, Dr Bell, wearing his bishop's robes beneath his overcoat. He ended by reading a poem by some famous poet about an airman who expected that he was going to die. One line I can remember: 'His country was Kiltartan Cross, his countrymen Kiltartan's poor', in which I instantly recognised Duncan.

The gathering was large, and included local people who were familiar and some who were not, for Mr Schwayder had seen that details of the service were published in the local papers in advance. Besides Mr Schwayder, and most of Goring Hall it seemed, there were in the gathering Mr Parker with a number of Sanders staff, the mayor of Worthing and some of the aldermen who had been at the ceremony on the tram, and even Sergeant-Major Kelly, recently released from East Grinstead Hospital having been fitted with a new leg by Mr McIndoe, the surgeon, who now also operated on cases at Goring Hall. Amazingly, and heaven knows how she found us, there, too, was Big Bertha and beside her our King's Counsel, very tall and thin. They stood, bareheaded in the sunshine, and their names appeared in the next morning's edition of the *Morning Post*, which reported much of the event. Also present was a contin-

163

gent from the Worthing Home Guard, as the Local Defence Volunteers were now called, who under the beady eye of the redoutable Sergeant Breakspear sang lustily during the hymns.

What the *Morning Post* did not report was a small incident which no one but myself could have noticed. It started trivially enough when halfway through the service a car drew up. I supposed to be carrying late-comers, therefore having heard it arrive I did not even turn my head. The last to arrive, it happened also that the car was the first to leave, and as it drew away I gasped in sudden recognition of the sound. I turned sharply and beheld Mother's Hispano-Suiza disappearing down the road. A man in a cap was driving and Mother sat next to him, wearing her cloche hat.

'Mother, Mother,' I ran shouting. But in vain: I was not seen.

Hattie and I decided that we did not wish to remain in her house, its associations having made it an uncomfortable place. We packed every-thing away and, to my own pang of disappoint-ment, Hattie went to Canterbury to live with her mother. She took Tiger with her and at first I missed him dreadfully, but I knew that this was best for him and that Mrs Brown would always look after him. Not long afterwards Hattie enlisted in the Wrens, which everyone said was just a reaction to the tragedy and that one day she would return to nursing.

As for myself, I started working again at Mr Schwayder's Field Hospital and became part of the duty roster, which meant that I also lived there, quartered in one of the Nissen huts. The hospital was understaffed and I worked as I had never done before, which gave me some distraction from what had gone before. In this way time passed quickly and for this I was grateful.

In the course of the work I often saw Mr Schwayder, who was now the director of the hospital, and there came a day when I found myself alone with him in the library, which he used as an office. I had been wondering about my future and evidently it had been on his mind as well for he settled down in a chair and waved me to another.

'You haf to decide, Villy, vat exactly you vill do with your life,' he began. 'For instance, do you vant to learn to drive ze trams?'

'No,' I replied. 'I don't think so. I think I've done with trams.'

'You are qvite right. I sink ze future vill be trolley buses, anyway. But zere are uzer zings vich you could do. Have you ever zought of becoming a doctor?'

'No,' I said. 'I don't think I would be clever enough, and anyway I haven't had nearly enough schooling.'

'Eeet is true zat you haf left school far too early, but I sink you vould be a good doctor. Let me talk to Mr McIndoe about it and zee vat you haf to do.'

I was touched that he had thought this out for me, and also wondered if he might be right. It was quite true that I had lost out in missing a proper education.

A short time later, one day when Mr McIndoe was finishing his weekly ward round, which I was allowed to follow, Mr Schwayder drew him aside.

'Don't you zink Villy vould make a good doctor, Archie?'

'Well, I am sure he would, Tibor,' replied Mr McIndoe, 'if you say so, but I don't think I know this Willy.' He paused. 'Oh, I see, you mean Fred.' That was the name I was known by on the wards. 'Certainly I do. I think he's exactly cut out to be a doctor.'

'Zen, Archie, perhaps you could tell us vat he has to do.'

'I will look into it, Tibor, certainly I will,' said Mr McIndoe.

My future having been thus decided by these two great and good men, I awaited with some interest and no little anxiety Mr McIndoe's further thoughts. They were not long in coming. Between the two of them it was decided that I should enrol as a part-time student at Worthing Technical College in order to take the School Certificate. I had to obtain credits in at least five subjects for matriculation, and when I had obtained them Mr McIndoe would arrange my admission to University College in London, since he operated at the hospital nearby. It was a case of do or die, and next day I enrolled. A year later at the examinations I obtained enough credits to pass matric and, to my surprise, also a distinction in Latin.

So I left Worthing and exchanged the familiar surroundings of Goring Hall, which was so strongly associated with both Duncan and Hattie, for the strange new world of London, the London of 1942, which was where my medical education began.

It was a troubled time, both for London and for me, and much water had to pass beneath the bridges before my education ended – if indeed it had an end. But that is another piece of history altogether.

Chapter Twenty

DAUNTING THOUGH THE prospects were to each of us in that period, nevertheless with the passage of time they became brighter and over the years the roseate glow of history also cast its spell. However, I did not appreciate this until later and now, at a time when the tram is part of a distant past, I find myself recalling it with real affection, something I seem to have communicated to others, to Duncan, for instance.

I must explain that Duncan is our eldest son, who arrived in the family when I had just become a doctor; in fact, he was more or less the celebration of that event. At the time he was born, his name was not even discussed, it being impossible to call him anything else, since we both knew that there simply had to be another Duncan.

That was twenty years ago and, I don't know why, it has taken Duncan, and also his brothers, all this time to discover that trams ran in the family the way they did, but perhaps their mother may have had something to do with it. The result is that, now they have found out about the two pound tram, they simply won't leave the subject alone. I do not complain, for of Duncan at this moment I am extremely proud for a reason I shall relate.

Their mother . . . But here I must go back to the beginning. I followed the plan of Mr Schwayder and Archie McIndoe and in due course found myself at the Royal Free Hospital in Gray's Inn Road, which is where I now work.

It was there, on the way to one of the wards, that I chanced to find myself walking behind a group of nurses, evidently probationers, for they wore the distinctive white caps made from a square of linen tied at the back with loose tails. One of the nurses looked different and some-how familiar; her cap was tied with a sort of uptilt that made it distinctly provocative. The thought shot through my mind that I had seen it somewhere before, and as I rounded the corner the recognition struck like lightning – it was

Hattie. The extraordinary coincidence that she should be working in the same hospital as myself struck me with the force of a bullet.

'Hattie,' I cried. 'I thought you were in the Wrens.'

'I was. Only I got an early demob to do nursing.'

Naturally we arranged to meet, and then one thing led to another so that after a while we began courting. We soon discovered that the same feelings were dormant in both our breasts and these were from our earliest days, even those at Canterbury. Therefore we scarcely spoke any words; our lives seamlessly united themselves and became one life, without a question asked or answered by either one of us. Thus it came about two years later when I qualified that we were wed, and as it started so it has continued.

We have been blessed with four sons, and the reason I am proud of Duncan is that he has just started his training course at St Mary's Hospital. In time, when he qualifies, he will be the latest in the tradition of our family, for both Mother's brothers who were killed were doctors, and before that there were three generations of them going back to Dr Isaac Cox of Honiton in Devonshire. He died of a heart attack while berating a carrier who was whipping his horse up a hill, and that was in 1825.

Chapter Twenty-One

WE OFTEN SPOKE OF the first Duncan and his times, which have seemed stranger still with the passage of the years, so that when, much later, we learned of the death of Mr Schwayder, and afterwards that of Mr Parker also, these seemed to be such milestones that we were filled with an urgent need to visit the places we associated with them, where their lives had made such an impact on our own. We already knew the parts of their stories that had been reported in the papers, but now we felt a need to find out more: all that we could before the traces vanished. This urge grew until the trail we imagined became a complete voyage into time past, and we started off one day the following May.

First we went to Acton and the Uxbridge Road and found the tramsheds, which had become a bus depot; and the Omnibus and Tramcar Company was now called London Transport. But of Alf, who after all had started us on trams, or even of anyone who knew him, we could find not a trace. A single totter came down the street driving an old Toyota pick-up which was the only reminder.

At this point we naturally had to go in search of Tiger, or rather Hambledown where he had retired, for Tiger himself had departed the scene long since. When Hattie enlisted in the Wrens her mother, Mrs Brown, had continued to care for Tiger until his death from natural causes at the age of fifteen. His total span was actually longer, for fifteen is not counting his time with the totters in Acton when he was growing up, before he acquired ourselves.

Therefore he had enjoyed a long retirement, in which he had plenty of time, no doubt, to recall the events or at least the smells of his salad days. Apparently, in his latter years he had chosen to spend most of his time out of doors, in all but the harshest months of the year, which I suppose is not surprising since that is where he would have started off. He was usually to be found in Mrs Brown's paddock, but we reflected that this was also not surprising, since that was where we had fought off the gang that had made so much trouble for us. We saw in a flashback that it was Tiger who had fetched Homer and caused him to gallop into the mob and scatter them.

So it was fitting that Mrs Brown had buried him in her paddock, marking his grave with a stick, and we went there to pay Tiger our last respects. Afterwards I arranged for the stick to be replaced by a stone carved with a Tiger. I pray that it is there still.

We visited Reigate but found that our friend Mr Parker had not stayed there for long, since evidently he had ambitions for greater things. Before the end of the war he had formed a partnership with an engineer by the name of Knoll, and between them they created a business manufacturing what was known as 'utility furniture' made from the bare minimum of raw materials, which was all that was available. Among their successes was the Parker-Knoll armchair, which swept the country in the years after the war. Thereafter his path became paved with gold. He made a series of acquisitions of department stores, culminating in a fierce contest for the ownership of Whiteleys of Bayswater, and by the end of his life he had become Sir Thomas Parker, the acknowledged prince of the retail industry.

Thereafter we took a train to Brighton and thence to Worthing, where we walked the length of the sea-front from Sayers to Sanders, but alas both had disappeared and of course so had the tramlines. At the site of Sanders a new supermarket was in the process of being built, and in a corner a McDonald's had already opened its doors. It seemed all too predictable. We hailed a taxi and asked the driver to take us to Goring Hall, where we felt familiarity might restore the balance in our journey of rediscovery. At first the cab driver hesitated but when I said 'Schwayder's Place' he seemed to understand. We drove at a slow pace, since the whole area that we had known as countryside now seemed to be built up. We recognised the Ilex Oak Avenue, or the part of it where we had once galloped the horses, and then the cab turned in to a large housing estate and soon the driver put us down on the corner of a road which he assured us was where we had asked for.

But of Goring Hall there was no trace, only a row of new houses and at the corner where we had alighted a newly erected road sign. Then we knew we had arrived for it bore the name 'Schwayder Place'.

We left as quickly as we could and made our way back to Worthing. We went to the local museum and asked for Mr Schwayder's butterfly collection but then, just as we entered the doorway, I saw the three enormous mahogany cabinets with their double rows of drawers which had once been so familiar. Obligingly the attendant unlocked them for us, remarking that no one seemed to bother to look at the butterflies these days, and he left us to it.

I went to the second cabinet and counted down to drawer twelve on the right, where I remembered that the Clouded Yellows started. The drawer was stiff, as though unused, and slightly swollen, but with careful pulling it opened and sure enough the Clouded Yellows were there in their neat rows. But each insect had its four wings lying separately on the white drawer bottom, while on its pin the remains of its body was still just visible. The camphor in the special recesses in each drawer back, of which the cabinet was redolent, had evidently not been successful. Mites had eaten the lot.

The next drawer and then the next were the same. Finally we came to our Vareefii with its double-spotted front wings, and the rear ones, all in a heap just like the others. I shut the drawer and found the attendant to return the key. He escorted us to the entrance.

'You know,' he said, 'that is a wonderful collection. It is a shame folks don't look at it these days. It must be ten years since I unlocked them last.'

'Yes,' I said. 'I realise that.'

A puzzled expression lingered on his face as we departed.

We groped our way into the sunlight which dazzled us and walked slowly till we reached the new pier, which was filled with holidaymakers, and then wandered along the front in the direction of Grand Avenue. We wished to look at the place where the old pier had stood, and where had been our tram, which was once our pride and joy. I have to admit that our experiences thus far had been so depressing that at this point our visions of the past had been all but extinguished; we were certainly not prepared for what came next.

The old pier stood there – all of it. It had been rebuilt in its full length, complete with the ballroom with its bright green dome at the sea end.

And at the head of the pier stood our tram.

It shone, the sunlight glistening on its crimson livery. Every coach line along the body caught it, and the driver's bold brass handle. Immaculate advertisements which now seemed curiously antique had been repainted to the smallest detail, giving it a splendour far greater, it must be said, than it had ever possessed in our day. We approached it with awe.

There were now iron railings around the pier and an entrance gate where there was a ticket booth. Near it was a small engraved sign, topped by the familiar oak leaves of the National Trust, on which was written: '*This tram and its restoration for the National Trust were the gift of T. Parker Esq.*'

We took our place in a line of sightseers, most of whom appeared to be Japanese, and in due course climbed the step at the entry by the driver's seat. The interior was just as immaculate as the outside, although it was difficult to appreciate all the details with such a press of people. A lady of the staff of the National Trust was trying her best to control the queue.

The driver's handle, the dials and lever, which were also brass, riveted our attention. Next we passed down the tram and there the Japanese tourists, students perhaps, one by one stopped at the front seat on the left where each took a photograph. Above the seat was a bronze plate inscribed with the words *'Tiger's place'*. We paused while we took it fully in.

The lady usher was quickly behind us. 'Do you want to take your picture of Tiger's place?' she asked.

'Yes, I certainly do,' I said. 'Only I've left my camera. Perhaps . . .'

'Then move along, please. There are others waiting.'

We returned home in a chastened mood, for the ghosts of the past had come back to haunt us and they were in no mood to go away.

The foremost of them was the ghost of the most extraordinary person of all, Tibor Schwayder. We knew much more about him now. He had been part of the Jewish exodus from Vienna after the First World War, and happily for him he left just before the inflation of the German mark, which of course would have deprived him of his fortune. This had been made in the years just before the war when he held a franchise for the newly invented American vacuum cleaner, the sole franchise for Europe at that time. The riches that resulted allowed him to retire, and probably most of his time thereafter had been spent travelling Europe in the pursuit of butterflies. I now know that in the world of entomology he had an international reputation, and very probably he never wished for anything else in his life but to be a retired country gentleman and to live in Sussex by the sea and enjoy his great collection.

He had brought with him from Vienna many remarkable objects of art, in particular the marvellous palace which he re-erected as Goring Hall, a building of the high Baroque brought in crates from a site near Vienna, where it had been dismantled. I realise now that it was modelled on Schönbrunn Palace in Vienna.

It could so easily have become the end of his purpose, where he might have lived out his life in contentment. But a new challenge arose and Tibor put the palace and his butterflies to one side and diverted all his energies to the country of his adoption in its life-and-death struggle with Hitler. And during all these events, amazingly, he had had time for us, for our tram and especially for Duncan, by whom he became quite obsessed.

Chapter Twenty-Two

THE WORLD IS CHANGING and the world around Gray's Inn Road, and the Royal Free Hospital, is changing faster than anywhere. *The Times* newspaper has left, and now we are about to move to Hampstead, where our brand-new hospital rises apace. With this enterprise I have from time to time been involved personally, as happened, for instance, when the foundation stone was laid.

On this occasion it fell to me, as dean of the Medical School, to escort the Queen Mother at the laying ceremony, for which I had to hand her a stainless-steel trowel, absurdly engraved by someone's misplaced effort with an outline of Buckingham Palace. Had I been able to do so, I would have given much to ask her if she re-membered, when she was Queen, the occasion of Duncan's receiving his decoration on the tram, but unfortunately it was not my position to open the conversation, least of all about a personal matter.

However, as it turned out, I had no need to worry, since she made the opening for me.

'Dr Scrutton,' she said, 'I believe that we may have met before. If I am right your brother was Duncan Scrutton. Is that the case?'

'Ma'am, I am proud to say that it is the case.'

'Then I wish you to know that the King treasured his meeting with your brother. In fact, my dear husband spoke of little else for several weeks.'

'Ma'am,' I murmured, 'thank you.' I could say no more, because all other words stuck in my throat.

This was at the beginning, for the building which she began now rises many floors high and looks over much of London, including the hospital in Gray's Inn Road. But I shall greatly miss the place where I have worked and lived for most of my adult life and which is filled with associations and memories. Now, as I look from my window, I see the green quadrangle, which has a single plane tree at its centre, and I reflect that that is where Hattie and I courted, which now seems a long time ago.

I stare from the window for a long time while I gather my thoughts together, and I am lost in wonder, not grief. Finally, I rise from my desk and put my papers in my case to take with me when I walk up the hill to our home.

I close the door behind me and lock it, and as I do so I look at the signboard on which is written: *Professor W. Scrutton, Department of Endocrinology*, and I wonder if they will take that and put it up in my new quarters, for I feel that it is part of me just as the Canterbury signboard belonged to Homer. It is evening, and I reflect that wherever I am going it will doubtless all be much the same.

I take from my pocket a small book which I carry with me and resort to reading at moments when I wish to regain peace of mind. It is a book of poems by the Roman poet Catullus, and it carries an English translation page by page across from the Latin.

I read the first two poems which are about his mistress's pet canary – or actually sparrow. The third poem is a sort of dedication to itself. It starts, 'Go forth little book into the world, and tell the world your story, for it is your life now.' For this one, the editor was kind enough to use my own translation.

The next poem, the 'Phasellus', is my favourite in the whole book. It is about a yacht which is built from pines on a mountainside above a lake. It is launched there and sails the seas of the world. Eventually it returns to the shore where it was built, and there rests and rots until finally it becomes a hulk.

Marvellous 'Phasellus'. But that is another tale.

A NOTE ON THE AUTHOR

The author is a retired doctor who lives in
Oxfordshire. This is his first book.

A NOTE ON THE TYPE

The text of this book is set in Bembo.
This type was first used in 1495 by the
Venetian printer Aldus Manutius for
Cardinal Bembo's *De Aetna*, and was cut for
Manutius by Francesco Griffo. It was one of
the types used by Claude Garamond
(1480–1561) as a model for his Romain de
L'Université, and so it was the forerunner
of what became standard European type
for the following two centuries. Its modern
form follows the original types and was
designed for Monotype in 1929.